SEVEN DAYS IN JUNE

A Novel by Alonzo Heath

COPYRIGHT

Alonzo A. Heath

Printed in the United States of America
First Printing: September 2013
Alpha B Creative edition published published 2020
Alpha B Creative Publishing

.

ISBN-13: 978-0-615-83575-4

DEDICATION

Bill, thank you for the Royal. You believed, when no one else did. I hope this makes you smile.

ACKNOWLEDGMENTS

I want to thank my children, Brandon, Brian and Ashleigh for encouraging me to become a better storyteller. I hope this meets your expectations.

BOOKS BY ALONZO HEATH

Seven Days in June

The Booster

The Braun Secret

DAY 1 - TUESDAY

The phone rang. I wasn't going to answer it because I was broke. It was 1983 – no caller ID, no cell phones – just an old rotary dial phone hanging from my kitchen wall. I didn't have an answering machine, so there was no way for me to screen my calls. And the odds were good that it was someone looking for money, that I didn't have. So, with no idea who was calling, I didn't answer it.

When it rang I was in my apartment, sitting on the couch in my living room, watching old reruns of Star Trek on my small black and white television.

"Maybe it's the bank," I muttered and turned the volume up on the TV. Ignoring bad news seemed to work well for me.

I had been floating checks around town and was nervous because I was close to being unable to cover them. Once the first bad check had hit the bank, an avalanche of checks drawn to my account would follow. If I didn't come up with the money to cover them in the next week or two, the City Prosecutor would file charges against me for writing bad paper.

However, I had to eat, I reasoned, and somehow concocted in my mind that what I was doing, despite the illegality, was justified. And for some strange reason I had an eerie confidence that at the right time luck would intervene.

So, I settled back onto the couch, and ignored the telephone. The silence was short-lived. The caller was persistent and seconds later, tried again.

"Okay," I said aloud. I jumped up from the couch, walked to the kitchen and grabbed the handset and angrily barked, "Hello."

1

"Bobby?" a startled voice asked.

I was relieved, because the caller was my stepfather, Harry. When I recognized his voice, I felt terrible that I had answered the phone so angrily because he was an extremely nice and pleasant person. He and my mother had married a year earlier. They were both widowers and had wed mostly out of convenience.

Harry had known my mom back in the nineteen-forties. They met shortly before World War II. At the time, she was married to Harry's best friend, Estevo Cardona. Estevo was her first husband. Harry had confessed to me that he had eyes for my mother back then but had never mentioned it to anyone. So, I suppose this whole marriage was one of convenience in my mother's eyes only. For Harry, it was a life-long dream.

I guess a storybook tale like that of Harry and my mom would have been kind of sweet in any other family. But my mother was one of those ball-busting matriarchs that made the notion of a happy ending a remote possibility.

Though controlling, and often verbally vicious, she was, nevertheless, a good mother. She loved her children unconditionally and would do anything within her means to make sure we were safe and protected. This however, was a courtesy that she extended only to her children.

But even in light of this, Harry maintained a calm and consistent demeanor. I had never seen him angry. It didn't matter what anyone said to him or how they said it; he always remained calm and even-keeled, which made him uniquely qualified to tolerate my mother.

"Oh, Harry. Hi. Sorry about that. But I never know who's calling," I started.

Harry saw right through me and said, "Bobby, if you need money, I'll send you money."

He was good like that and was always happy to offer his help. However, my mother raised me to be independent and to work things out, if possible, on my own. And that was how I operated. I typically didn't accept charity from anyone, unless I had no other options.

"You know I appreciate that. But, I'm good. I've got some things in the works right now, and I think I'll be okay," I lied.

"You know the offer is there if you need it," he pressed.

I always liked Harry. When I was a kid, I used to cut his grass and do odd jobs around his house. At that time, his wife, Theresa - a very strange lady - was still alive. And even though I was comfortable around Harry, when I was around Theresa Bremen, it was a different story. An older, short lady, as thin as a rail, with a head full of gray hair, she sat on the porch during the summer, chain-smoking, and watched as I cut their grass. She neither spoke nor smiled. She simply glared at me the entire time. If I spoke to her, she ignored me. So I worked as fast as I could just to get away from her.

When I finished though, Harry would invite me to his back yard and we'd sit in his lawn chairs and have a cold drink. He would enjoy a beer and I would sip on a cola. Harry would sometimes tell me stories about the folk he ran around with in the thirties and the forties. He told of his days as a roadie for some of the biggest jazz and swing bands of the era. I didn't know if everything he said was the truth, but he managed to tell such a fascinating story that I really didn't care.

"I'm good, Harry. So, are you and mom okay?" I asked, sensing that his call might have something to do with her.

"Your mother is fine but she's giving me hell because I'm not feeling well this week. With your sister graduating from the university on Friday, well, she's scared I'm not going to recover in time to take her down to the ceremony. And I was wondering..."

"No problem," I interrupted, "I'll come home and drive you and Mom to the graduation," I said, gladly volunteering my services.

Harry had been diagnosed with some sort of cancer a few months earlier but was vague as to what type of cancer. When I pressed him about it, he just said, "A man needs to keep some things to himself." I figured it had something to do with his male plumbing, and he was embarrassed to discuss it. So I let it go.

But my mom wouldn't. The cancer slowed Harry a bit. And along with the residual effects from a stroke that he had suffered two years previous, he didn't get around as well as when he was healthier.

3

This brought the worse out in my mother. Even though I felt he got around fine, my mother always complained that he was, "halfway crippled and too damned slow."

"I'll wire you some money for the bus," he offered.

"That's okay, Harry, I've got it covered. I have enough money to take care of the ticket. It's still early so I should be able to make the afternoon bus. I'll be there this evening," I said, even though I didn't have the money or any idea how to raise the money for a bus ticket in such a short time.

"Listen, Bobby, I appreciate what you're doing so you have to let me do something for you. I'll wire one hundred dollars to the telegraph office - which I believe is at the bus station. That way, I'll feel better about this," he insisted. I nearly jumped out of my shoes because for me, one hundred dollars was a king's ransom. With it, I'd be able to buy my ticket and cover my overdrafts.

Harry knew me well, and he was one of the few people from whom I would accept charity. Since I had returned to college, after a stint in the army, it seemed that I was always broke. I wanted to get my degree and end my perpetual cycle in poverty, but the lack of money made my commitment to finish difficult. But Harry and my mother were both solidly behind my decision to get my undergraduate degree, and were always there to help financially.

"Okay, Harry, if it'll make you feel better. Hey, can you pick me up at the bus station when I get to town?"

"Sure, I'll be there, Bobby."

"Maybe we can have a couple of beers tonight," I suggested.

"I'll hold you to that," he laughed.

"All right then, I'll see you this evening," I ended and hung up the phone.

I went back into the living room and turned off the television. Then I ran upstairs and quickly threw a bunch of dirty clothes into my old army duffle bag, stuffed a few toiletries inside and left my apartment.

When I stepped outside the heat almost knocked me over. "Awful hot for June," I noticed, tossed my duffel over my shoulder and headed to the bus station.

***

The telegraph guy was a dick. He had worked at the office in the bus station for as long as I could remember, and had always been a dick. However, travelers suffered him, including I, because he stood between us and our money.

This wasn't my first dealing with him. I had been to his window before, and even then, he had made it difficult for me to get my money and keep my cool. He was one of those people that seemed to have it in for everyone. He carried a chip on his shoulder the size of a two by four. I suspected he must have been teased and bullied everyday as a child to turn into such an asshole. I guess he felt he needed to pass the misery he suffered on to others.

I went up to the window. He was shielded from the public by a thick, bullet-proof glass. His eyes were fixed on a magazine.

"What?" he snapped.

"I've got money," I answered.

"I need identification," he said. His eyes remained focused on the magazine.

He was a rude son-of-a-bitch. I didn't like him and really would have liked to kick in the door to the office, and pound the shit out of his fat ass. But that wouldn't have got me my money. So, like everyone else, I took his shit and stood silently by while I handed my driver's license to him. He looked at it, looked at me, and returned it.

"I need a second form of I.D."

"Why do I need to give you another form of I.D.? The telegraph company doesn't require two forms of I.D. to pick up money."

"I'm the company. And today, I need two forms of identification," he said.

"Look, man..." Then I stopped and recomposed myself. "Okay, here's my student I.D." I slid it under the window.

He looked it over then asked, "Do you have a major credit card? Anyone can get one of these." He handed it back to me.

I was getting pissed. "Look, I'm not trying to cause a problem, and I

5

know you are doing your job. I'm just trying to get my money."

"That's not my problem. I can't accept this second form of I.D."

We had danced this dance before. I knew that ultimately I would lose so I decided to just cut through the chase and get the deal done. "Okay, I'm sorry. I have to catch the next bus home, and I really need to pick up the eighty dollars my family sent me."

"Eighty dollars, huh?" he asked and nervously shuffled some paperwork. He glanced out the window around the terminal. "Okay, don't worry about the other form of identification. I'm satisfied you are who you say you are."

"Thank you."

"Are you sure it was only eighty bucks?" he reiterated.

I sighed. "Yes, I'm sure. It was just eighty bucks."

He smiled. "Okay, sign at the bottom of the form there," he said and slid the paper under the window.

I signed it and watched as he opened the cash drawer, took out five twenty-dollar bills, and then slipped one into his pocket. He slid the remaining bills under the glass and went about his work.

It was useless to protest. At that point in my life, the cards were stacked against me. I didn't have anything, and like so many others, I was preyed upon and taken advantage of by those in positions of power. The twenty dollars were simply a tax for being poor.

He'd get his one day, I reasoned, and shoved the money into my pocket. I walked over to the ticket counter and purchased a ticket on a bus that was leaving in fifteen minutes.

"Better hurry," the clerk warned and handed me my change.

The departure doors were behind me, on the other side of the terminal. I turned to head toward them but when I took my first step, someone grabbed me.

I tried to pull away, but as I came around I saw that it was a transportation police officer who was holding on to me. I had a sinking feeling. Most of my encounters with the police didn't go well. Innocent or not, they always seemed to have probable cause, especially the transportation police. They were notorious for finding shit that didn't exist before they arrived.

"I'm sorry, officer," I nervously apologized.

"You haven't done anything wrong," he started with a smile, "I just need to ask you a quick question."

"Well, my bus is coming, and I don't want to miss it," I stuttered. It was refreshing running across a good cop for once.

"Don't worry, young man, it won't take long."

"Okay, yes sir, officer. Anything I can do to help."

"You just received money from the telegraph clerk, correct?"

"Yes, I did."

"We've had some complaints. Did he make you pay a vig to get your money?" he asked.

So finally someone had caught this fucker and now I had the opportunity to nail his ass to the wall. I looked back toward the telegraph office, and I saw that another officer had detained the clerk. They were anxiously looking in my direction.

I had him. I could do the world a favor and turn him in. But instead, I turned back to the policeman who had stopped me and said, "No, officer, he didn't charge me anything to get my money. He gave me all that I was due," I lied. I had a bus to catch. I didn't have time for statements, courts, or anything related to the criminal-justice system. Besides, the odds were good that he would beat the charge and be right back on the job the following week. And of course, with my luck, I would have to deal with him again.

"Are you sure?" The officer pressed.

"Yes sir, I'm sure. He was straight up honest with me."

The officer turned to his partner holding the clerk, and waved. The other officer released him. The clerk smiled and went back into his office.

I thought for a moment that he smiled because I had done him a solid. But he probably smiled because once again, he had beaten the system. I knew he would be back to his old ways as soon as I stepped onto the bus.

"Is that all, officer?" I asked.

The officer laughed. "You know that's bullshit," he accused.

"Well, maybe, but it's my reality," I answered.

"I understand. Have a safe trip," he nodded and walked off.

I arrived at my gate just in time to board my bus. I threw my duffle into the luggage compartment and climbed aboard. I settled into a comfortable window seat near the front and fell asleep.

***

Harry was there when I stepped off the bus. He sat in his green Chrysler, his head barely visible above the dash, and waited on me. He wore his trademark gray fedora. I grabbed my duffel bag and walked over to the car.

When I arrived at the car, he smiled, got out and opened the trunk. I tossed my bag into it and gave him a hug.

"Hey, Harry," I greeted. "It's good to see you."

Until I met Harry, I had considered myself short at five feet ten inches. Standing next to him, though, I felt like a towering giant. However, his diminutive stature and gentle nature in no way took away from his toughness. His years in the mill, forging steel, had left him powerfully strong; which I felt every time we shook hands.

I genuinely liked Harry. He was a kind man and had always treated my siblings and me very well. His short frame was accentuated by the extra pounds he carried around his belly. But his round face beamed an uncommon kindness for someone who was around my mother twenty-four hours a day. He always wore a fedora and looked as though he had stepped out of the fifties. He loved his hats.

"I'm good today. We'll see what tomorrow will bring," he said and handed me the keys.

"Where's the Chevy?" I asked. Harry had recently bought a brand new 1983 Chevrolet Malibu.

"It's at the shop. I'm having it serviced," he explained.

"When will it be ready?"

"We'll pick it up on the way home," he said, "if that's okay with you."

"Sure, it's no problem," I agreed. "Who's at the house?"

"Your mom's there, that's for sure," he sighed, "and Stephanie and Tanya.

They tell me that Denise is on her way as well."

I sensed the frustration in his voice. I understood where it was coming from. Stephanie was my oldest sister, eight years my senior. Tanya, my niece, was her daughter. She was only nine, but had this irritating habit of hanging around grown-ups. Stephanie and Tanya – along with my mother – could easily fray the nerves of even the most stoic, steely person. Tanya was spoiled rotten. She was her only grandchild, and Mom doted over her.

Stephanie was a drunkard. It was one thing, I have to admit, that she did well. When she drank all bets were off as to what would come out of her mouth. Usually it was a profanity laced rant full of lies and accusations.

Denise was two years older than I and far less of a problem than my mother or Stephanie. She had her moments, but for the most part, she was a caring person. Normally, Denise wouldn't allow herself to be dragged into the family frays and arguments, but if she was pressed and cornered, she came out swinging. She was fiercely combative and capable of verbally taking down anyone in her way. That didn't happen often, though.

"I thought Stephanie and Denise were already in Columbus for the graduation. Why is everyone coming here first?"

"I don't know, Bobby. But it's going to be crowded driving down to Columbus tomorrow with a car load. Stephanie and Tanya showed up on the bus yesterday. A friend is supposed to drop Denise off tonight or tomorrow," Harry explained.

My family – especially my sister, Stephanie - had a way of converging uninvited on the unsuspecting at the last minute. She would show up, unannounced, as though it was normal behavior. But I suspected on this visit she had an agenda. She brought her daughter, Tanya, to whom my mother could not say "no". Stephanie was definitely up to something.

"Don't sweat it, Harry. I'll make sure they behave."

"I'm glad someone will, because I don't seem to have much influence in my own house," he lamented with a smile.

I heard him loud and clear. Despite his smile, his saddened tone betrayed him.

"Don't let them stress you," I consoled and quickly changed the subject.

9

"Why don't we stop and get some beer?"

"Okay, we'll get beer," he smiled and then fell silent.

He wasn't happy. Harry wasn't one that could deal with the idiosyncrasies of a large family like mine. He and his first wife never had children. Dealing with my large, unpredictably crazy family was something for which he was unprepared. I thought maybe if he had known what lie ahead for him when he came courting my mother, he would have run away screaming. But then I realized that Harry was pure goodness and undeterred. He would have come calling anyways.

Whenever my mother was around, even when Harry's first wife was alive, he looked at my mom with longing eyes. But as far as I knew, he never said a word to anyone about it while he was with his first wife, Theresa.

After Theresa Bremen had died, he came courting. I think my mom might have been amused by the whole thing; she seemed to like the idea of Harry coming by and keeping her company because she was an empty-nester. We were all either in college or living on our own. So, it seemed that the courtship and subsequent marriage made sense.

But when I heard about it, I approached the news with skepticism simply because of my mother's toughness and stormy history with other men. She could be very difficult, and I wasn't sure Harry knew this.

My mother Sarah was a tough lady. Both divorced and widowed once, she was a single mother more by choice than by anything. She didn't tolerate any man who wouldn't immediately acquiesce to her ways and ideas. During the time I had lived under her roof, there were never divergent opinions or challenges to her authority. What she said was the gospel. You either accepted it or you left.

And so when this union occurred, I felt sorry for Harry. He was a quiet and non-assuming man. He had a beautiful laugh and a wonderful smile. He was gentle with a sensitive soul. Harry was no match for my mother, regardless of how much he loved her. It wouldn't be long before she began to tear him down, piece by piece, until there was nothing left of him. And the tone in his voice suggested to me that my mother had already begun her demolition project.

***

I pulled the Chrysler into the driveway. Harry parked the Malibu behind me. I had barely shut the engine off and opened the car door when I heard Stephanie. Her voice blasted through the screen from the opened kitchen window and filled the outdoor air. She was already well on her way to getting liquored up.

"I'll tell you this," I heard her slur, "if that fucker thinks he's going to get away with this shit, he has another thought coming."

I had no idea what or whom she was talking about, but apparently my mother did because she responded, "Shut up, they just got here."

Stephanie's language surprised me; not that she would curse, because when she was well-oiled, she could curse out anyone. But to use these words around my mother - who played the devout Christian to the tee – was somewhat dangerous. But since she was my mother's favorite daughter, she received a pass.

Based on what I had already heard it was evident that some conspiracy or other type of dramatic shit was afoot and apparently it somehow involved Harry and me.

When I set foot onto the front porch, I suddenly became the prodigal son returning home for a visit. I guessed that Mom felt I had gone deaf since my last visit and hadn't heard Stephanie cursing up a storm when I got out of the car. In a way, it was pathetic as to how transparent they were, but since I failed to protest, I encouraged their bad behavior.

My mother ran to the door and screamed, "Here's my baby," just as I stepped inside. She gave me a slight hug, but nothing overly affectionate.

I loved my mom. And I'm sure she loved me. But I was also her least favorite because I often failed to walk the line. So, I knew that if I were on a sinking ship with my family, and my mother had one too few life preservers, well, no more Bobby. Besides, she didn't waste her affections on renegades.

"Is that my baby brother?" Stephanie asked, in her 'I'm soon to be drunk' voice, from the kitchen. She came out and tried to give me a hug. The strong odor of alcohol hit me in the face well before her arms fell around my shoulders. She pulled me close. "Hi, Bobby."

"Hi, Stephanie," I greeted, pulling away from her as quickly as possible. I looked around the living room and noticed that my mother had already left the room. Apparently, announcing the fact that her son was home was enough affection for one day. It must have been tiring for her.

Harry followed me into the house and amid the slight ruckus created by my appearance, was completely ignored.

Harry was happy with that. I had observed on more than one occasion that he preferred quiet anonymity when my sisters and brothers were around. And quite frankly, when my family would get together, I wasn't sure if Harry wanted any of us around, including me. Harry and I had a good relationship, but my family and their actions strained that as well.

I wasn't a saint, by any stretch of the imagination. I had my bad moments with my friends, family and even Harry. There were times when my family would do something low-down, and I would respond by going lower. But, through it all, I can say, without any reservations that I wasn't disingenuous like the rest of my family. I only wanted Harry's friendship – and nothing more.

"By the way," Stephanie interrupted, "if you think you are going to get that car, well, you're wrong," she slurred.

"What?" I questioned. "Where did that come from? Exactly, what car are you talking about?"

Harry headed straight for his bedroom. Whatever was getting ready to be said, apparently he didn't want to hear it. I was on my own. I thought about calling him back but it was too late. He closed the bedroom door down the hall, before I could call out to him.

"Hush, girl," my mom said to Stephanie. "It's not the time to talk about that. Besides, I need to discuss it with Harry."

It was easy to decipher the drunken talk. Now that Harry had purchased a new car, Stephanie wanted his old car.

"I don't want Harry's car," I said.

"Yeah, right. I saw you drive up in that green car and I know you want it," Stephanie accused. She often went on brief detours from her brain when she was drinking.

"I drove up in the Chrysler because Harry couldn't drive two cars at one time," I explained. But I quickly realized that Stephanie wasn't in any condition for a rational conversation. She was officially drunk.

"Well, you're not going to get it because I need that car for Tanya and me."

I couldn't resist though, getting at least one jab in. "You and Tanya, my ass. You need a car for you and that loser boyfriend of yours."

"If you think…"

"Shut up," I interrupted, "I don't want the car. That's a conversation you need to have with Harry," I said, grabbed my duffle bag and escaped to the basement.

***

Vivian was one beautiful young lady. But her boyfriend, Jimmy, was absolutely crazy. I didn't know who invited Vivian to the house but whoever it was probably didn't know that Vivian could mean trouble for me. While I liked her, I tried to steer clear of her.

I was in the basement, lying on the couch and enjoying the cooler air, when she came bouncing down the stairs and greeted me in her high-pitched, exceptionally girlie voice, "When did you get home?"

There was one point in my life, when I had been absolutely crazy about Vivian. But even though I wanted to keep our friendship intact, for now I just wanted to keep a healthy distance from her. So before she could converge on me with hugs and kisses, I stood, stopped her short of my face and said, "I'm busy, Viv. You need to leave."

I had dated Vivian in high school and thought that she might be the one. That was until Jimmy came along and forced himself into the picture and suggested that I break off my relationship with her.

Jimmy was a bully. No question about it. And Jimmy got what Jimmy wanted. If you refused Jimmy, he would beat the shit out of you. I simply

13

gave Jimmy what he wanted and lived to fight another day.

So when Jimmy came to me and suggested I step aside, I had little choice but to oblige. What complicated matters was that Jimmy and I were good friends. For some reason, many years earlier, he had taken a liking to me and I became one of his trusted confidants. I got along well with him.

I didn't tell Vivian that I broke up with her because of Jimmy. Had I done that, she would have never spoken to me again. I told her it was because I had decided to join the Army. Which I ultimately did.

Since our break-up, Vivian and I still maintained a relationship. But she was one of those overly affectionate people that liked to kiss and hug and I was scared that Jimmy would take it the wrong way.

So, on this day, I wasn't going to let her get me into any shit with Jimmy. I put a stop to it right away.

"Oh, Bobby, why are you being this way?" she protested, knocked my hands away and gave me a kiss on the cheek.

"Vivian, just go. If Jimmy finds out you're here, all hell is going to break loose."

"Jimmy doesn't own me," she whined, trying to take my hand. "Besides, you are my friend, my Bobby, and I haven't seen you in nearly two months."

"He may not own you, but he believes in his mind that he does and that's good enough for me. So, turn around, go back up those stairs and leave," I insisted.

This wasn't going to be easy.

"You know you want me here," she said, taking a seat on the couch. She was wearing a white knit halter top, and I could see her nipples through the stitching. At any other time this would have tempted me, but the thought of Jimmy loomed large in my decision to defer any romantic appeal that I may have had. I decided to go with being safe.

"Look, Vivian, please leave. I'm serious. You really need to go."

Then, as if cued, my mother yelled from upstairs.

"Bobby, there's someone here to see you."

I didn't need to go upstairs. I knew exactly who wanted to see me. It was Jimmy. I was sure of it. "You see, he followed you over here."

Vivian laughed. "How do you even know it's him?"

"Who else could it be? Hell, I don't have any friends here anymore – just you and Jimmy. And now, with you being here, that's in jeopardy. Fuck," I yelled and headed for the stairs.

"Bobby," my mom called out again.

"Okay, I'm coming," I said and turned to Vivian, "If he hurts me, I swear..." I started, but couldn't think of anything to threaten her with, so I just turned and climbed the stairs.

"Your friend is at the door," my mom said to me when I reached the top of the stairs. I walked through the kitchen, into the living room and over to the front door. I peered through the screen. It was Jimmy. My stomach sank.

"Vivian's here, isn't she?" he asked.

Jimmy was one of those people whose appearance was as threatening as his deep voice. Muscles just seemed to bulge from everywhere and when he opened his mouth he spoke in such a deep, scary voice and manner, that one could not help but walk away with a twinge of fear.

"Yeah, Jimmy," I answered, a bit scared. I pushed the door open to let him in. "She's in the basement."

Jimmy smiled. "Good. I'm glad she's with you. I was worried for a moment that she was out fucking around on me."

Jimmy knew the house well. He had visited with me before and together we had smoked a few joints in the basement while my mother and Harry were out. So, he walked past me without hesitation.

But as we neared the stairs leading to the basement, out of seemingly nowhere Harry came careening around the corner. He abruptly grabbed Jimmy by the arm, a step or two from the basement's door.

"Where do you think you're going?" he yelled angrily.

I didn't know what was going on, but my instincts told me to act quickly. Jimmy didn't like to be touched and while he was for the most part respectful of older people, I wasn't sure how he would take being grabbed. I was stunned that Harry had suddenly flipped out. His tone was angry and his behavior atypical of what I would have expected from him.

15

"I'm sorry, man," Jimmy apologized and jerked away from Harry. "I was just going downstairs to get my girlfriend."

By now, my sister and mother made their way into the kitchen to witness the commotion.

"Harry, it's cool," I offered, trying to calm him down. I thought it might have been the medication that caused him to act this way. But, he didn't discuss his health problems with me in any detail, so I was unsure of what kind of medication he might have been on and the potential side effects. Since this was so uncharacteristic of him, I had to pin this unexpected episode on medication.

"I don't want this thug in my house," Harry screamed at Jimmy.

He got the thug piece right, so apparently he was familiar with Jimmy and his antics. But, Harry wasn't confrontational. He was a kind and quiet man. This was uncharacteristic of him.

"Look, old dude," Jimmy started, "I don't know what your beef with me might be, but I'm just here to pick up my girlfriend. She's visiting with Bobby."

During the commotion, Vivian had found her way up the stairs and stopped in the middle of the kitchen and witnessed some of the argument. She took Jimmy's other arm and whispered, "Let's just go, Jimmy."

It was clear that Jimmy was angry, and although he stood squarely in the middle of another man's home, he wasn't going to retreat so easily. He pulled his arm away from Vivian.

"No, the old guy has a problem with me, and I want to know why," he insisted.

My mom and sister, who were witnessing the exchange, remained uncharacteristically quiet.

"I told you to get out of my damn house," Harry screamed, the veins bulging from his temple. I had never seen him this angry.

I tried to calm him and said, "Harry, seriously, Jimmy is okay," but he glared at me until I voluntarily backed off.

Harry turned to Jimmy and persisted. "He's a damn crook. He stole my tools. I saw him do it just the other night."

"Look, man, I don't know what the hell you're talking about," Jimmy started, and turned to me. "Bobby, you need to get the old dude under control. I'm patient, but only to a point."

"You're a thief and I want to know where my tools are," Harry screamed, angrily shaking his fist at Jimmy.

Jimmy made two fists of his own, and I saw his forearms flex. He looked as though he was ready to deck Harry. "Man, I don't know what you are talking about..."

I tried to intervene again, and took a step toward Harry. But as I neared him, he jammed his hand into right pants pocket and pulled out a small caliber pistol and began to wave it in the air.

As though synchronized my mother yelled, "Old Lord," while my older sister Stephanie screamed, "He's got a gun."

Jimmy stepped back. "Now cool it, mister. I don't want any trouble."

For a moment, I froze. Even though I had carried a gun as a military policeman in the army for three years, they still scared the hell out of me, especially when in someone else's hand. However, I thought I could talk Harry down. "Harry, please, put the gun away," I pleaded.

"Bobby, your friend stole my tools, and if he doesn't give them back to me, I'll shoot him right here where he stands," Harry threatened.

Jimmy looked over at me, a little unnerved. Bravado had its limits, and Jimmy's had ended when he found the barrel of the handgun just inches from his face. "Honestly, Bobby, I have no idea what he's talking about."

"It's the medication," my mother snapped. "It makes him crazy."

"Shut up, woman," Harry yelled turning to my mom. "Don't call me crazy."

Then my mom did something amazingly stupid but impressively courageous. She walked over to Harry, and without hesitation, grabbed the gun from his hand and said, "Look, I don't know who the hell you think you are, but don't you ever wave a gun around my children or in my face again."

She turned and handed the gun to me.

Harry slumped over and walked out of the room and fell solemnly onto the couch.

"I'm sorry, Jimmy," I apologized. The entire sequence of events just happened so fast. My mother was absolutely incredible and unnerved.

"Hey, this shit is too deep for me," Jimmy started and turned to Vivian, "Come on, let's get the fuck out of this crazy house."

Vivian quickly obliged and ran across the kitchen floor and took his hand. "I'll see you later, Bobby," she said. Jimmy pulled on her arms and led her toward the front door.

"Later, Bobby," he said to me and mumbled something to Vivian as they left through the front door.

My mother turned, glared at Harry sitting on the couch, and went to their bedroom.

"Crazy," Stephanie muttered under her breath and went to the guest bedroom with Tanya.

***

Harry sat on the couch by himself. His hands were at his sides, and he seemed to be staring at me. I realized, as I walked over to him, he was almost in a trance, staring blankly into space.

I sat in the chair next to the couch. "So, Harry, what's up, man? That wasn't you."

Harry wore glasses and they darkened somewhat in the dim lighting. I could barely see his eyes. He looked at me and then turned away and stared at the wall for a few minutes before he finally spoke. "Bobby, I don't know what happened. I just lost my head and snapped. I've seen your friend before, and he has a reputation, but I have no idea why I accused him of stealing my tools."

He shook his head and appeared confused by the entire incident.

"No harm, Harry. Jimmy's not the type to hold a grudge, and something tells me this isn't the first time someone has held a gun on him," I laughed.

Harry couldn't force a smile. "Bobby, what's wrong with me? I lost my mind in there. I'm always in pain. Every part of my body seems to hurt. And the medication just doesn't do any good."

"Did they give you pills for the pain?" I asked. This was the most he had ever said about his condition. I believed that he was on medication for some type of cancer, but I wasn't sure because he had never confirmed it. I suspected though, if it were cancer, it was progressing more rapidly now.

"Yes, they gave me pills, but they don't do much good. It hurts so badly sometimes. I do the best I can to deal with the pain."

"What's causing the pain?"

"It's the cancer. This is the first time in my life that I can't get well. It's eating me up inside, and I'm finding it difficult just to do simple things. I never thought my life would come to this."

I felt for him. Not only did he have to deal with my ball busting mother, but sadly, he had to face this pain, and I believed the inevitability that he would not get any better. "Is there anything I can do to help out?" I offered.

"I don't see what you can do, Bobby. You have always been kind to me and honestly, I can't think of anything else. Unless you know a doctor..."

"Hey, maybe we can go up to the Cleveland Clinic. They may have a treatment for what you have." It was brilliant on my part, I thought. "Heck, Harry, if the Cleveland Clinic was good enough for the Shah of Iran, it has to be the place to go. Maybe they can help."

While I let my youthful enthusiasm run on, Harry didn't appear as optimistic. He forced a smile. "Well, maybe they will. Why don't you take some time after your summer semester ends, and we can go up one day in August and afterwards, catch an Indians game," he suggested.

Harry was going to die soon from his cancer. I knew this and had to accept it. It was difficult to look at him, once a proud, powerful man, now just a shell of his former self. Sadly, though, the cancer seemed more debilitating on his mind than his body. He had lost his hope, and this hurt me the most.

"Sounds like a good idea to me, Harry. When I'm all done with school for the summer, we'll ride," I agreed, and quickly changed the subject and said, "Hey, why don't you get some rest and tomorrow we can install the screens on the windows and doors."

Harry briefly balked at my suggestion. He stayed glued to his seat. I knew he was hesitant to go back to the room and deal with my mother.

19

"Look, mom's bark is worse than her bite," I teased. "You ought to know this by now."

"I do, but sometimes her bark is pretty damn nasty and hard to deal with."

"This is true. But hey, you've only been dealing with it for a year. I've had to put up with her for over twenty years now," I laughed.

"I see your point. Oh well, I guess I'll go to bed. I don't want to keep you up."

"It's not a problem, Harry. I appreciate all that you do for me and the family."

He stood up and stretched. He turned to me and said, "You know I didn't promise your sister that car? If you want it, I'll give it to you."

I smiled. "I don't want the car. I appreciate your offer, but you'd have hell to pay, if you gave it to me. And of course, I'd have hell to pay if I accepted it."

"But if you want it, I'll give it to you," he reiterated. "Hell, if you want the new one, I'll give that one to you."

"Keep your cars, okay," I laughed. "You're not going to pawn them off on me so that I will have to chauffeur my mom around. That's your job, man."

Harry laughed along with me. "Thanks for everything, Bobby. You're a good kid."

I was flattered. "You don't know the half of it. If you knew me you would see that I have a lot of work to do before I can be canonized."

"Nevertheless, I think you are a good young man. Oh well," he said, taking in a deep breath and letting it out, "I've put it off long enough. I guess it's time to go face the music."

I smiled and said, "Good night." Then I remembered. "Oh, Harry, here," I handed him his pistol.

Harry smiled, took the gun and then limped his way down the hall, favoring his left side. He turned the door knob and sneaked into the room. As soon as the door closed, my mom started in on him. I could hear her giving him hell for his earlier antics.

I walked halfway down the hall to the linen closet and pulled out a blanket and a pillow. I tossed the pillow on the couch, kicked my shoes off, and then laid down for the night. I pulled the blanket over me and heard my mother still going after Harry.

"Poor Harry," I muttered, closed my eyes, and drifted off to sleep.

DAY 2 - WEDNESDAY

The front door flew open, and the screen door slammed behind it. The commotion startled me from my peaceful repose on the couch. I was in one of those dreams that found me in a wonderful place, and it felt as though someone had jerked me by the arm and violently pulled me out of my bliss into a sobering, less beautiful reality.

The culprit was my brother Richard - we called him Dickie - bursting into the house and making one of his grand, unplanned entrances.

I grabbed my blanket and threw it over my lap. Dickie grinned when he saw what I had done. Without even a greeting he laughed and said, "Morning stiffy, eh?"

I gave him the finger and grasped the blanket more tightly as my momentary embarrassment subsided to its natural state. "Hey, Dickie," I grumbled and looked around to make sure no one else had noticed my embarrassment.

My mother was in the kitchen. I looked up at the wall clock in the living room. "Seven o'clock, shit, do you people sleep?" I complained and reclined back onto the couch.

"Early bird gets the worm," Dickie sang and headed for the kitchen.

"Oh, Dickie," my mother greeted and for the next ten minutes made all sorts of fuss over him. She called out to me a couple of times to ask, "Have you seen Dickie?" and I just wanted to throw up. How the fuck could I have not seen him when he walked right past me?

While Stephanie was my mother's favorite child, Dickie ran a very close second. In fact, sometimes, based on the way she showered him with affection, it seemed he was her favorite. Dickie did his part to earn that love by playing the perfect child role to a tee. He filled her head full of his 'success' bullshit, and she fell for it hook, line and sinker. Mom always made such a fuss over Dickie, and I was sure that it would break her heart if she knew the truth about him.

Dickie is my oldest brother. He was born in 1948 and had just turned thirty five years old in May of 1983.

"So, did you spend last night at a hotel?" I asked when he came back into the living room from the kitchen.

"Leave Dickie alone," my mother interrupted. "He's tired because of the long drive." She followed him in the room and sat next to him on the love seat.

Dickie smiled at me with his perfect, signing bonus teeth. When he graduated from high school in the late sixties, he was a very talented baseball player. He went on to play in college and was drafted by a professional baseball team in the nineteen seventies in the early rounds. He used his signing bonus to fix his mouth.

Unfortunately, Dickie's ego was bigger than his talent, and it wasn't long before he was released. He settled in Chicago and made up this cockamamie story about working for the Cook County Commissioner's Office. My mom believed his story, but the rest of us knew it was bullshit. We didn't quite know what he did for a living, but somehow he managed.

"I drove down this morning," he said and turned to mom and gave her a hug.

I nodded because I knew it was a bullshit answer. Chicago was a six-hour drive from our hometown. It was seven in the morning. He had to leave around 1:00 am. He was usually so stoned out of his mind by that time in the morning, it would have been impossible for him to make the drive. There was another story here that I was sure would unfold during his visit. "Yeah, okay, Dickie."

"Oh, you don't believe me?" he asked, standing and coming threateningly towards me on the couch. Dickie wasn't someone to be messed with. He could easily beat the shit out of me. He was blessed with a disciplined workout ethic that resulted in a powerful frame – ripped in all the right places; while I was the proverbial 98 pound weakling – well not 98 pounds, but skinny, nevertheless. One of his arms could crush me.

My problem was sarcasm. And that sarcasm often got me into trouble. "No, I believe you, Dickie," I corrected, waving him off. He sat back down.

"Now, boys," my mother began, "Be good today. Your sister is graduating this week, and we don't want anything to take away from her moment."

"It's okay, Momma," Dickie said. "So, Bobby, you want to take a ride with me after you get dressed."

I was reasonably sure that during the ride, the "rest of the story" would unfold. "All right. I'll ride."

Harry's house was quite small so everyone heard everything. As soon as I agreed to go with Dickie one of the bedroom doors opened from down the hall, and Harry emerged.

He lumbered out to the living room and stared for a minute.

Dickie nodded, "Hey, Harry."

"Dickie," Harry responded. Dickie and Harry didn't like each other, and that was about the best they were going to do. Harry turned to me. "You still want to help me with those screens?"

"Sure do, Harry," I answered.

"Well I was thinking about doing them this morning. Will you be back soon?"

"I will. This probably won't take long. Let me get dressed and I'll do this with Dickie and then when I come back we can put them in."

"Are you sure you and Richard will be finished with your business?"

"Pretty sure, Harry," I answered. I noticed that Harry had the same clothes on from the day before, and hadn't shaved yet, which wasn't like him.

I had thought my mother was an early riser until I spent my first night in Harry's house. My mother would get up about 6:00 or 6:30. But Harry was usually walking around at 5:00 am. It didn't matter what time he went to bed; he was always up by 5:00 in the morning.

And normally at this time of day he was dressed, shaved, and had already started the day's work.

"Are you okay, Harry?" I asked. His dress and hygiene concerned me, and I thought the drugs may have been kicking in again. He didn't seem disoriented or strange, but I certainly didn't want to see a repeat of what had happened the day before.

"I'm fine, Bobby. You go take care of your business with your brother and when you are done, let me know," he said and returned to the bedroom, closing the door behind him.

"Who knows what's wrong with that crazy man," my mother muttered, slapping Dickie on the leg. They both laughed.

"He's a good man, Momma," I defended. "He's not crazy and you should quit calling him that."

"You're always defending him. I think you love him more than you love me," she complained.

"Well I love you, Momma," Dickie interrupted, giving her a hug.

"I'm taking my bath," I groaned, got up from the couch, grabbed my duffel and went to the bathroom.

***

"How much money do you have?" Dickie asked as he drove past the high school. We had left the house a little more than twenty minutes earlier, and until now, he hadn't said a word.

"I'm broke, man. I have maybe five or ten bucks. That's it."

Dickie pulled in front of the high school and brought the car to a stop. "That's where all the magic happened," he said, almost in a whisper. "The touchdowns, the homeruns, the winning baskets. Yep, that's where I made my name." He turned to me. "So, you don't have any more cash stashed away?" he asked.

"I'm tapped, Dickie. I don't have any money. Harry wired me a few bucks just to get a bus ticket home so that I can take him and Mom to Laura's graduation."

It was my youngest sister, Laura, who was graduating from Ohio State with a degree in Economics. She had always been studious and committed. Our mom expected the entire family to be at the graduation.

"You think maybe Harry will front me some money?" he asked.

I laughed. "When hell freezes over."

"Not funny."

"What kind of money do you need?" I asked.

"At least a grand."

"Shit, Dickie, you may as well go and rob a bank."

"I may have to," he said, started the car and pulled away from the high school.

We drove in silence for a few minutes until Dickie broke in and asked, "Are you sure Harry won't give me any money?"

"I'm reasonably sure, Dickie. You can ask him, but I don't think he will. He's not the type to lend money."

"He gave you some money to get home," Dickie noted.

"For one it wasn't a grand. And secondly, he needed me to come home," I explained. I knew, though, that if I needed money and asked Harry for it, he would give it to me. I didn't know why he would do this for me. After all, at this point in my life, I hadn't done anything to give him any indicator that I was serious about turning my life around.

Dickie was another story. Harry just didn't like him. And that would probably be the primary reason he wouldn't give him any money.

"Yeah, well I guess that's probably right," he muttered.

"What do you need a thousand bucks for?" I asked.

"Got some trouble."

"What kind of trouble are you in, Dickie?" I knew the answer before I asked the question. He owed money to either a drug dealer or loan shark.

"Just some trouble..." and in mid-sentence, we were interrupted by a siren. I looked into the side-view mirror and saw flashing lights behind us.

"Shit, Dickie, why are they pulling us over?" I asked in disgust.

"Just keep quiet and let me handle this," he snapped as two police officers exited the cruiser. The one coming to my side of the car reached down and unsnapped his holster. Then the other officer screamed out Dickie's name.

"Dickie Foster," he yelled and hurried towards the car. You would have thought he just saw the President of the United States.

Dickie smiled. "Looks like a fan," he muttered to me and exited the vehicle, just as the other officer arrived at my window and nodded for me to exit the vehicle.

I got out of the car, and the officer pushed me up against the vehicle and frisked me.

"He's okay," his partner yelled from the other side of the car, fully engaged in a conversation with Dickie.

He released me and said, "Sorry, but have to be careful."

"No problem, officer," I said, relieved, that despite the appearance of an impropriety by my brother, we fortunately had been pulled over by a friendly, but clueless, police officer.

"You know, Dickie, this car is reported as stolen," the officer said.

"Are you serious?" Dickie started. "That woman. She's a little pissed with me, so I guess this is her way of getting back at me," he explained.

"Women," the officer started, "can't live with them, can't live without them, and…"

"Can't shoot them," Dickie joined in, both howling.

I looked at the other police officer and we both shook our heads.

Now I understood. My brother had either stolen the car or taken it – a late model Cadillac – without permission. However, athletes in my hometown always seemed to get a pass. While Dickie probably should have been in handcuffs and headed off to jail, instead he was bullshitting with the cop about the good old days, and signing an autograph. Of course, I wasn't too sanctimonious, because had this played out the way it should have, the police officers probably would have arrested me for some type of complicity in Dickie's crime.

"Look, just get it straightened out with the owner and come by the station tomorrow, and we'll get this resolved," the officer said and shook his hand. "Take care of yourself, Dickie."

I got back in the car as the cruiser pulled away. "Stolen, Dickie?"

"Yeah, but it's not like that. I just have to ditch the car. I should have done it yesterday, but I got caught up in this business."

"Ditch the car? What the fuck do you mean by that?"

"Look, a buddy of mine is having some financial difficulties. I told him I was coming to Ohio, and he gave me the keys to the car and told me to drive it to Cleveland, leave the keys in it and walk away. He would report it as stolen. But that was yesterday," Dickie explained.

I couldn't believe Dickie and some of the crazy shit he got himself involved in. "So what are you going to do now?"

"Well now, I'm going to drop you off at the house, make my way to Cleveland to ditch this Caddy, and then disappear for a while."

"So, you're not coming to Laura's graduation?"

"No, I can't. Once I ditch the car, I have to keep a low profile. Since I can't come up with the money I have to make myself scarce."

"Dickie, what are you involved in?"

"Don't worry about it, Bobby. I'll be okay. I need you to smooth this over with Momma when you get back home. Just tell her that I had to run some errands."

"She's going to be crushed; and probably pissed."

"She won't be pissed at me," he said, "But I expect she will be a little disappointed. I'll call her this afternoon and make up some bullshit."

"When will you be back around?"

"When things cool down. I don't know how long that's going to take."

"Well, be careful, okay?"

"You know me," he smiled.

"Yeah, I do know you, and that's why I'm asking you to be careful."

***

My mother wasn't happy that Dickie didn't come back with me. I think in her heart, she knew he had skipped town but she didn't express it aloud. I was happy, though, to see that Harry had changed his clothes and shaved. He was even smiling. I thought that maybe the source of the smile had to do with Dickie's departure.

It was only ten in the morning when Dickie had dropped me off at the house . That gave Harry and me enough time to install the screens in the windows. When I walked into the house, Harry had already taken the screens out of storage and left them propped against the couch. He was ready to get to work.

I was impressed, because of late, Harry had shown quite a bit of disinterest in most things. He had become somewhat lethargic. But this morning though, I was seeing a renewed spirit from him and a beaming smile and a hop to his gait. Harry seemed to be genuinely happy today. I walked over and grabbed the screens.

"I'll take these outside," I offered.

"You do that, Bobby and I'll go get the step ladder," he said, and headed to the basement.

Stephanie, Tanya and my mother were sitting around the kitchen table having a cup of coffee. I thought it strange that a ten-year-old girl was sitting with her mother and grandmother, drinking coffee and listening to the latest gossip.

"Momma, I'm taking these screens outside. If you need me, I'll be out there with Harry installing them."

"Well, I'm amazed," she started and took a sip of her coffee, "that you can get that old crippled man to work. He doesn't do anything around here."

Stephanie laughed.

"Grandpa Harry is crippled," Tanya teased, singing it as though a song.

This sickened me. Harry was having one of his best days in recent memory, and these three had to do their part to ruin it.

"You three deserve each other," I snapped in disgust, grabbed the screens and walked out of the house.

I hated when they did this. Harry was a good man, but he was slowing down like all men in their late sixties and early seventies. Apparently, either they didn't understand, or care, that their behavior was crass and hurtful. But it didn't matter how many times I argued or corrected; they would continue to do it. They just weren't very nice people at all.

I was sure that Harry had heard what they said, because when he returned from the basement, carrying the step ladder, his beaming smile had disappeared. A sullen look had replaced his happier face. Clearly, he wasn't pleased with my mother, sister and niece. He walked past them with a glare.

I met him in the kitchen, took the ladder and carried it to the side of the house and set it up. Harry followed me with the screens.

"You better climb the ladder, Bobby, because an old crippled man can't…"

"Stop that, Harry," I snapped. "Just stop it now. Don't pay any attention to them. They're full of shit."

Harry smiled. "Well, this is what I hear all the time, Bobby, and quite frankly, it hurts."

"My mother is a ball buster. That's her M.O. and has always been her M.O. So, don't let that kind of stuff poison your mind."

"Okay, Bobby. Where did your brother go?" he asked, handing me the screen.

I hated when he did this. "Harry, you can't keep this inside. Don't slough this shit off like it's not important. Let her know that this is bullshit."

"Bobby, it's okay, all right. Now, where did your brother go?"

I didn't press any further. "I'm not sure where he went, but he told me this morning that he needed a bunch of money."

"How much is he looking for?"

I pushed the screen into place and descended the ladder. "He said he needed a thousand bucks." I grabbed the ladder and walked along the side of the house to the next window.

"A thousand bucks? What kind of trouble is he in, now?"

"I don't know. But I think he needs it pretty quickly to repay some type of debt."

"You think someone is after him?"

I scaled the step ladder, and Harry handed me the screen. "I'm sure of it. But he wouldn't tell me what he was involved in." I snapped the screen into place, jumped off the ladder and folded it closed.

"Well, maybe I should loan him the money."

"That's your call. But you know if you give him that money, it's not a loan.

You'll never see it again."

"But if something were to happen to your brother, and I could have prevented it, I would never be able to live with that."

I looked toward the back of the house and realized that our small step ladder wasn't going to work for the remaining windows. They were too high. Harry had built this ranch styled home on the side of a hill. The front of the house, at the top of the hill and street level, was easily accessible with the step ladder. But the windows in the rear were too high for a step ladder, and a conventional ladder was needed. I didn't think it mattered though, because at this point, Harry was tired.

"Look, Harry, you do what you think is right. It's your money."

"What would you do?" he asked.

"He's my brother and I wouldn't want anything to happen to him."

"When you hear from him, tell him that I'll help."

"That's the problem – when I hear from him. I'm not sure where he is and when he's going to surface again."

"He'll surface," Harry said, then took a deep breath. "I'm tired. Why don't we have one of those beers that you bought yesterday?"

"Okay, hold on and I will run in and grab a few."

When I walked into the kitchen, the mean bitches club was still having a meeting. I didn't know what was going through my mother's head, but she had been exceptionally edgy the past day or so and extremely bitchy.

"Where are you going with those beers?" my mother asked, as I grabbed them from the refrigerator.

"You'd better not drink them all," Stephanie butted in.

"What are you talking about Steph? These aren't your beers. I bought them yesterday."

"I assumed," she said, standing, and walking toward me, "that you bought them for everyone here. Not just for yourself and old ass Harry."

She snatched one of the beers from my hand.

"Look, if you want a beer, drink a beer. In fact, drink them all if you'd like. Besides being a whore, drinking is the only other talent you have."

"Fuck you," she snapped and took her seat at the table.

31

"Hey," my mother screamed. "I've had enough of this bickering, arguing and cursing. You two stop it right now."

"I have too much respect for Mama to tell you how I really feel," I said, grabbed four beers and joined Harry on the front lawn.

When I returned, I noticed that Harry had unfolded two lawn chairs under the oak tree. It was near noon, and the tree provided nice shading from what was shaping up to be a very hot and humid day. He sat with his back to the house, facing the street.

I laughed, handed him a beer and sat next to him. "You know that ignoring the crazies inside is not going to make this situation any better."

Harry glared at me and said, "Bobby, don't say things like that about your family. You're better than that."

"I'm sorry. It's just that they can be so difficult sometimes..."

Harry chuckled and took a sip of his beer and said, "Don't I know."

The tree's leaves rustled above us, and we got a brief break from the hot afternoon sun. Harry leaned back in the chair, tilted his head skyward and closed his eyes as the breeze danced around us. When it had passed, he opened his eyes and took another drink of his beer.

He had always been a man of few words, but today I noticed that he seemed a bit off.

He spoke. "Tell your friend I'm sorry that I pulled a gun on him last night. I don't know what came over me."

"Don't worry about it. Jimmy won't hold a grudge. But I have to admit, that was a little strange. Are you feeling better today?"

Harry took a sip of his beer and answered, "I'm okay today, though your mother has been a little rough on me."

"I don't know how you put up with this type of treatment. You're a better man than I. Plus, it seems that lately she's been a little snippy."

"Yes, she has. But she's concerned about your sister's graduation. I wish though, she would go a little easier on me. I'm doing the best I can."

"What's the doctor saying?" I didn't expect him to answer. And true to form, he didn't. Harry changed the subject.

"Bobby, what do you think would really make your mother happy?"

"I'm not sure anyone can answer that question, Harry. I don't even think that Mom can. Sometimes I believe that she keeps moving the finish line on purpose. Just when you think you have her figured out, she moves it back a little further, and you have to run a little longer. So, I do feel for you. But hey, don't take her to heart. That's just her way."

"Don't make excuses for bad behavior. I treat your mother well. I take care of her the best that she will allow me. Yet through it all, I'm an old crippled man. I move too slowly. I'm always tired."

"This can drive you crazy if you let it, Harry."

"Yes, I know. But I appreciate the fact that you take the time to listen to an old man complain," he smiled and fell quiet for a few minutes.

He wasn't okay. He was far from it. He was tired - both physically and mentally. His fight with cancer was wearing his body down while my mom destroyed his mind and spirit. Through it all, though, I'd never heard him scream, yell, or even raise his voice at either my mother or any of her children. The episode with Jimmy, the previous evening, was a rare aberration. Harry was a good man, and I was proud that he was my step-father.

"You know, Bobby," he began, "I'm starting to get tired again. This beer is working on me."

"Are you going to be okay?" I asked.

"I should probably lie down for about an hour, and we can pick up on this project later this afternoon."

"You want me to wake you?" I offered.

"No, I'll be okay. I just need to rest for an hour or so."

"Okay. I'll come in, too," I said. I figured that soon we would lose our shade anyway so I followed him into the house.

When Harry stepped through the front door, my mother walked up to him and took his hand and crammed some folded cash into it.

"Here," she said, "this is your money."

"What money?" he stammered.

"The money for the phone bill," my mom snapped.

I was absolutely clueless about what was going on. But I saw Stephanie, sitting in a chair in the corner of the living room, snickering.

Harry glanced over at her. He took the money, crammed it in his pocket, lowered his head and went toward his bedroom, down the hall, on the left.

He opened the door to the bedroom and paused for a moment. He turned and looked down the hall toward me and smiled. When I returned the smile, he went into the room. As his bedroom door closed, I said, "Just an hour, Harry. We've got work to do."

***

"What was that all about?" I asked my mother, after Harry had disappeared into the bedroom.

"What are you talking about?"

"That money you crammed into his hand. What's with you, Mom? Why do you do some of the things you do?"

"That money was for my half of the telephone bill. He kept bothering me about paying my share, so I gave it to him."

"That's how you do that? You cram the money into his hands to embarrass him in front of the family? You're lucky he agreed to split it because most of the charges belong to you. You shouldn't embarrass him like that."

"Oh he's just so cheap. And here you are defending him over me, your own mother. I wanted to embarrass him. I wanted you children to see how cheap he can be."

"I don't get it. If you agreed to split the bill with him, and he asked for the money to pay the bill, how can you call him cheap? You know Harry would've paid the whole damn thing if that was your agreement. But you agreed to split it with him. So why would you ridicule him like that? Sometimes you are unbelievable."

I didn't think Stephanie would stand by silently while I went after our mother. Predictably, she joined in with, "You need to leave Mom alone. Harry is a cheap old man. He can't take it with him, can he?"

"Why do you two just always gang up on him? He's a good man."

34

"Good man, my ass," Stephanie snapped.

"I don't need to hear this," I said, turned and walked out of the room, down the hallway, to the guest bedroom opposite Harry's room. I figured I could take a nap until Harry felt better. But when my hand touched the door knob, it happened.

Before I took one step into the bedroom, I heard a loud "pop." It was as though someone had set off a firecracker in the house. I froze momentarily and in that instant, I felt something fly past the bottom of my pants leg. I looked down just as an object lodged into the baseboard, sending splinters flying into the air.

A sense of uneasiness came over me, just as I realized that what I had heard was the unmistakable sound of a gun, that had been discharged inside the house. And it was a bullet that flew past my leg and lodged into the baseboard. The sound, and bullet, came from Harry's room.

My stomach sank. "My God," I thought. Something very bad had just happened. At first I thought maybe Harry had lost his mind and had gone ape shit in his room and discharged a weapon. But as I stood and listened from the hallway, I didn't hear any sounds coming from his room.

Under normal circumstances, a random shooting would have scared me into flight. But this wasn't random. I was reasonably sure that Harry had shot himself.

I stood frozen in the hallway, trying to come to terms with what I believed had happened, and at the same time, trying to figure out what to do next. While part of me just wanted to walk out the house, leave and never look back on this sadness, Harry meant too much to me. At that moment, I made the decision to herd everyone out of the house and onto the front lawn, but my mother screamed from the kitchen.

She came barreling around the corner and charged towards me. I grabbed her by the arm and said as gently as I could, "Mama, everyone needs to get out the house, now."

She resisted, but I tightened my grip. Stephanie soon followed into the hallway and Tanya, who had been outside playing, opened the front door and tried to walk inside. But before she had placed one foot onto the living-room carpet, I yelled, "Everyone, please, get outside, now."

It was all happening so fast. I wanted to check on Harry, but I needed to move everyone outside first.

"Please, Mom, I'll explain in a moment. But for now, you have to get outside. That was a gunshot. For your own protection, please go outside now."

Mom and Stephanie complied. Stephanie grabbed Tanya by the arm and dragged her across the porch and onto the front lawn, at a safe distance from the house. My mother hurried outside just a step or two behind them.

Once they were a safe distance from the house, I turned and walked down the hall to Harry's room. I tapped softly on the door and whispered, "Harry."

I tried two more times but there was no answer. At that point I had no choice but to assume that Harry must have shot himself. The thought saddened me, but I didn't have time to grieve. I reached for the door knob and readied myself to enter Harry's bedroom. But I decided not to because I thought it would be best if the police were the first to enter the bedroom.

I turned and walked back toward the kitchen. The house was empty - the only noise coming from the television in the living room. I walked into the kitchen. Above the sink were two small windows that looked out over the front lawn. I peered through the windows and saw my mother, Stephanie, and Tanya, huddled together, near the car. I reached for the telephone, on the wall next to me, and dialed the police.

My family, especially Dickie, knew quite a few police officers in our small town. Some, we had grown up with and others we came to know through Dickie's athletic accomplishments. So we were in good standing; however, I still didn't want them to send a random officer to the house. I wanted someone that I knew to respond to the scene. So when the dispatcher answered I said, "I need to speak to Jackson."

Fred Jackson was a friend of the family. We had known him forever, and I felt that he would be the perfect police officer to respond to this tragedy.

"This is Officer Jackson," a male voice answered.

"Fred, this is Bobby Foster. Can you come to my house. I think my stepfather just shot himself."

There was a pause. "Harry?"

"Yeah."

"Did you touch anything, Bobby?"

"Not a thing, Fred. He's in his room."

"All right. I'll send EMTs, and I'll be there in about five minutes. Don't go into the room and don't touch anything," he instructed and hung up the phone.

I put the receiver back onto the base and walked out the kitchen, through the living room, and exited the house through the front door.

"What's happening?" my mother asked, rushing toward me as I stepped onto the grass.

"Jackson is on the way. The emergency squad should be here, shortly."

My mother looked up to the sky and said, "Oh Lord, what has that old fool done now?"

I shook my head and frowned at her. "Look, stay here until Fred says it's okay to go back into the house," I said and then walked toward the front door.

I needed to call Doug, my other brother.

***

Doug was quiet and reserved. Fiercely loyal to the family, he was normally non-controversial and kept his opinions and thoughts to himself. He had decided to settle in our home town after college, and lived only a few minutes away from my mother and Harry.

When I told him what I suspected had happened, he simply said, "Uh huh."

I gave him a few more details, and he told me that he would be on his way.

I waited for maybe two or three minutes inside the kitchen until Doug pulled up to the house. As he exited his car, I heard the sound of sirens, in the distance.

I met Doug in the living room, just as he stepped inside the door. He walked toward me. Doug was a little shorter than I, but otherwise, it was easy to tell that we were brothers.

"So what's going on now?" he asked.

"I'm waiting for Jackson to arrive. I think he should be here any moment," I answered, just as the emergency squad pulled up in front of the house. Officer Jackson pulled up right behind them and jumped out of his police cruiser and hurried toward the front door.

Doug and I met him on the porch.

"Okay, show me where he is," he said.

I led Fred into the house and down the hallway. Doug followed us inside. When I came to the room, I nodded to Fred, "In there."

"Okay, step to the side," he requested and knocked on the door. "Harry, this is Fred Jackson. Are you okay?"

There was no answer. Jackson tried again and asked, "Harry, are you okay?" He knocked on the door once more.

Fred grabbed the door knob, turned it and gently pushed the door open. He looked inside, then closed the door and turned to us and shook his head.

He grabbed his radio. "What's the ETA on the EMT's?" he asked.

"They are on the way," the dispatcher's answer blared throughout the house.

"It looks like he shot himself in the head. He's still alive, but barely. The ambulance should be here shortly. You may want to go out and prepare your mom. This is bad."

I looked over at my brother who dropped his head. I turned to Fred Jackson. "Fred, I need to see him," I said.

"Are you sure? It's a mess in there," he cautioned.

"I'm sure. I have to see him."

"Okay, hurry," he agreed and stepped to the side and opened the door.

Harry was lying on the floor, near the foot of the bed. His arms were sprawled to his side. Near his right hand, which was palm up, lay a small caliber Baretta. His head was lying in a puddle of blood. His eyes were closed, but oddly, although lying crooked on his face, his glasses were still on.

The sadness I experienced as I stepped inside the room and over to Harry nearly overwhelmed me. My heart ached, and I did all I could to fight back the tears. Ultimately, though, as I knelt next to him and watched his chest slowly rise up and down, the tears gently streamed from my eyes and down my cheeks.

"It's okay, Harry," I said, doing my best to comfort him. I took his left hand and squeezed it. I could feel him respond with a light grip. He was there, but he was leaving me. I wanted to ask why and to plead with him to fight this and stay. But I knew he was drifting away. And all I could manage to say, through my tears, was simply, "I love you, Harry."

The EMTs entered the room and ushered me to the side. I took one last glance at Harry then turned to walk out the room. I could have sworn, as I looked down at him, for one brief moment, he managed to grin.

When I turned away to leave the room, I noticed a wad of money sitting on the dresser. It was the money my mother had given to Harry for the telephone bill. It lay there, on the dresser, as though put there by a man who had just experienced the final insult. He hadn't bothered to secure it. He simply sat it, still in a wad, on the dresser. In all the years I had known Harry, I had never seen him leave money sitting around.

I walked through the room and out of the door. Doug was standing in the living room, watching the commotion as the EMTs brought in a stretcher. I walked over to him. "Did you tell them yet?" I asked.

"Nope. I thought it was something you could do," he answered and looked away from me.

Doug, as I said, was non-confrontational. Even in that solemn moment, he shied away from telling my mother the truth. I suspected he felt that since Harry had shot himself, she wouldn't take it well, and he didn't want to deal with that.

"All right, Doug. I'll do it," I sighed, and walked out of the house into the afternoon sun.

My mother was standing by the ambulance, patiently waiting. Stephanie and Tanya were standing in the driveway, talking to a neighbor, who had come outside during the commotion. They were, though, within earshot of my mother, so they would hear me break the news.

"Mama," I started, as I neared her, "Harry's shot himself. He's still alive, but he is not doing well."

My mother remained quiet for a moment. However, as soon as Stephanie heard the words, she let out a loud shriek and screamed at the top of her lungs, "Oh Lord. My daddy has killed himself. Oh, Lord, he's dead."

I ignored her. Tanya looked amused as she watched her mother make an apparent fool of herself by dancing around the lawn, waving her hands in the air and feigning grief. I knew Stephanie well enough to know that she wasn't doing this out of sadness or loss. She was doing this for show.

"Stop that foolishness," Mom said angrily to her. My mother, always as tough as nails, didn't tolerate emotional outbursts of any kind in public.

Stephanie, though, continued her antics.

"I said to stop it, damn it," my mother snapped with a glare. This time Stephanie got the message and shut up immediately.

"Mama, do you understand what I'm saying?" I asked.

"Of course I understand. That old fool shot himself the day before your sister graduates. How could he do such a selfish thing?" she snapped.

"Mom, come on. Harry is dying. How can you say that?" I asked.

"Leave me be. I want to be alone," she said and turned away from me.

"Whatever makes you happy," I agreed, and walked back toward the house just as the medics opened the door and started to bring Harry out, strapped to the gurney.

When they pulled him down the two stairs leading from the porch and onto the walkway, one of the medics looked up and asked, "Who's riding with us?"

I looked over at my mother who seemed to be ignoring the question. She didn't say anything. I walked over to her. "Mama, did you hear the man? You need to go with them."

She put her head down and spoke quietly, "I'm not going. I don't have time for this. Your sister will graduate tomorrow and I swear before God, I will be there to see her do so. I'm not going to let Harry's craziness ruin her graduation."

"Mama, Harry shot himself. You need to go with him to the hospital," I said and looked up as the EMTs began to load Harry into the back of the ambulance.

"I'm not going," she insisted, a determined look on her face.

I was at a loss, but I knew one thing would motivate my mother to get into the back of the ambulance. And so I said it. "Listen, if anyone finds out you didn't go with your dying husband to the hospital can you imagine the scandal?"

That was enough to get my mother into the back of the squad. She pulled herself up, walked to the back of the ambulance and in her phoniest voice said, "I'm coming, Harry. I'm coming."

The ambulance pulled away. I stood there, stunned, and listened to the siren until its drone trailed off in the distance.

I was going to miss Harry. The way he took his life left me confused. I didn't know if he was trying to make a statement, send a message or whatever. But he chose to take his life at a time when his wife and stepchildren were in the house with him.

I guessed his hurt was greater than he could bear.

***

I stood for a few minutes in the front yard and blankly stared down the street. Everything was just so unbelievable. I joined my family inside the house.

It wasn't long after the ambulance had departed with Harry, that we went into his room and cleaned it. Doug took on the most difficult task and wiped the blood from the floor. After he finished, we searched the room, and frantically looked for some piece of paper, a bit of an explanation, anything that would indicate why he chose that day and time to end his life. But he didn't leave a note.

Oddly, the entire evening was spent in an eerie silence. We were all stunned and dumbfounded. It was strange spending a night in Harry's house without him. We didn't talk much about it. We just wondered why.

But apparently Harry decided to reciprocate his cruel treatment with a cruelty of his own – he would leave us wondering why, for the rest of our lives.

After we were done cleaning and contemplating, I went to the back yard and waited for my mother to return with the inevitable news. I sat on the picnic table, watched the sun set, and waited for official notification that Harry had died.

When my mother returned from the hospital with the news, I moved my vigil to the front yard, where hours before Harry and I had enjoyed a beer together. I sat in the very same lawn chair and remained there all night until the morning sun peaked over the tree tops.

DAY 3 - THURSDAY

My neck hurt, and my knees were sore from sleeping in the lawn chair. It was strange that my family – especially my mother – would let me sleep outside on the front lawn all night. I would have thought someone would have come out and checked on me. Apparently they, too, were grappling with what had happened and had their own personal demons to exorcise.

I got up and stretched and looked around the quiet neighborhood. It was still early so no one was out. I turned and went inside the house.

Doug had decided to spend the night and was fast asleep on the couch. I walked past him, and into the kitchen where I found my mother sitting at the kitchen table sipping on a cup of coffee.

I opened the refrigerator and pulled out a cola and joined her. "Good morning, Ma," I said and sat down.

"Good morning, baby," she greeted, staring contemplatively at her cup of coffee and saucer.

"Did you sleep?" I asked her.

"Yes, I slept okay. Not restful, just okay," she answered.

"I'm having a hard time with this. I can't believe Harry did such a thing," I said.

"Well he did," she murmured and took another sip of her coffee.

"He was in a lot of pain," I said. I had my theories as to why Harry had shot himself but it wasn't the time to bring them up. My mother, despite her hard exterior, did have a sensitive side. She kept that side of herself well hidden, so it didn't come out often. But on this morning, while we were at the table contemplating the previous day's events, I could see some emotion slip out.

"I'm sure he was, honey. You want breakfast?" she offered.

"I'll just have a couple of slices of toast after my shower. Don't fix anything for me."

"I don't mind, Bobby."

"That's okay, Mama. The others will be up soon, and maybe they'll want something to eat. I think I'll go take my shower before everyone starts stirring," I said. As I started to walk away my mother called out.

"Bobby," she said softly. I stopped and turned to her. "Yes ma'am."

"Do you think he loved me?" she asked.

"He did, Mama. I'm sure of it. With all of his heart."

"Then why did he do this?"

I walked over to my mother and gave her a hug. "Mama, he loved you. I don't know why he did what he did, but I am sure he loved you. He told me often. Maybe he just didn't understand you; I don't know." No one understood my mother. Not even her children. To me, it was pretty clear why Harry took his own life. But she couldn't see it. And I left it that way.

I gave her a kiss on the forehead and went to take my shower.

***

I hadn't been out of the bathroom more than five minutes when the doorbell rang, a few minutes past eight in the morning. My brother Doug stirred, but turned away from the door and curled up on the couch to continue his rest.

"Shit," I muttered when I saw him turn away from the door.

"Who could that be?" my mom asked from the kitchen. She had already started cooking a full breakfast of eggs, biscuits, sausage and hash browns.

I walked over to the door and opened it and was greeted by John C. Spencer. John – J.C. as we called him - owned a mortuary in our town. I had known him most of my life – in fact, I went to school with his children. He was a tall, heavy set, fair-skinned man with a booming voice. He always wore a suit and hat. "How are you doing this morning, young man," he greeted with a smile as I opened the door.

J.C. didn't wait for me to invite him into the house, choosing instead to barge past me. "Is your mother home?" he asked as he entered the living room.

"She's in the kitchen..." I started. He knew his way around the house. His funeral home had handled the arrangements for Harry's first wife. So, he headed directly for the kitchen before I could finish my sentence.

"Oh, is that Sarah's good cooking I smell?" he bellowed as he entered the kitchen. "Sarah, I am so sorry for your loss."

He walked over to my mother and gave her a hug. I wasn't surprised that he was here. This was his way. In some respects, I guess I preferred that he dealt with friends in this manner. Death can be confusing. We didn't exactly know which way to turn or what to do next. J.C. was helpful in that regard. However, there was also an unseemly nature to his approach. Coming to the homes of the recently departed to sell his goods and services had a seedy, cheap taint to it.

J.C. removed his hat and sat down at the kitchen table. My mother leaned over and gave him a kiss on the cheek. "Thanks for coming by, J.C. Can I fix you a plate?" she offered.

"I can't pass up an opportunity to eat some of Sarah Bremen's good home cooking," he said.

Doesn't look as if you've passed up on many meals, I said to myself. I was indifferent about J.C. I wasn't sure if I really liked him or not. He always seemed to come on too strong. Plus, he was a mortician. That in itself, was a turn-off for me.

I had already guessed that his unexpected visit was because of Harry. And apparently my mother had expected his visit as well because she said, "I suspect you will need to go by the hospital and pick him up."

"It's already been taken care of, Sarah. The hospital released the body to me after the coroner signed off. He's over at the funeral home now. I didn't think you would want to leave him at the hospital. I'll gladly transport him to any funeral home you want," he offered.

It was awful bold of J.C., I thought. This wasn't like picking up someone's

45

dry cleaning in anticipation that he would be asked to do so. This was a body. But though he was an undertaker, he was also a salesman - and apparently a very good one.

"Nonsense, J.C., you take care of Harry. Thank you for moving him to your place," my mom said and fell silent as she fixed J.C. a plate.

"Sarah," J.C. began, and cleared his throat. I knew what was coming. Even though he was a friend, J.C. was first and foremost a businessman. "Because of Harry's untimely death I'm sure that financial matters are the last thing on your mind..."

"Don't fret J.C.," my mother interrupted, "I'll go to the bank today and take out whatever you need to give him a good burial. Just call me with the details when you get back to the funeral home."

"Don't you want to come down and pick out something nice for him?" J.C. asked.

"No, I think I'll let Bobby do that. I've got too many things on my mind."

I couldn't imagine what was more important than this, but I suspected this was my penance for liking and getting along with Harry. Since she deferred the arrangements to me, I had heard enough. I walked out the front door, turned and walked along the side of the house to the backyard. The front of the house faced the east, so the rear of the house, at this time of the morning, cast a wonderful shadow on the back yard, creating a cool relief from the sun.

Harry had put a picnic table near the back door. I sat on it, my back to the house and stared toward the end of the property line. A breeze gently massaged my face as I sat and thought about the events, thus far.

The past twenty-four hours were difficult. I was mournful, but I couldn't grieve. For some reason, the impact of the tragedy hadn't hit me. With everything moving so fast – J.C. discussing the details – it was difficult to bring myself to the point of grief.

"Hey, little brother," a voice rang out. It was my sister Denise. She put her hands on my shoulders and gave me a kiss on the cheek.

"Are you okay?" she asked, and walked around the table to face me. I was surprised to see her. Denise was short, like my mother, but the similarities ended there. Unlike my mother, she was still thin, but more importantly, came across as a kinder, more caring person.

I smiled. It was good to see her. "Yeah, I'm okay. When did you get here?"

"My friend dropped me off a few minutes ago."

"Your friend?" I said with a smile.

"It's not like that. He's just a good friend," she giggled and her mood quickly changed. "I didn't know anything until Ma filled me in just now. How could this happen?"

She climbed onto the table and took a seat next to me.

"I don't know, Sis. One minute we were working on the screens and then, before I knew it, he was gone."

"Did anything provoke it?"

"Maybe it was the painkillers; I just don't know," I said. But I did know or at least I had a theory. I couldn't tell Denise because even though she was pretty even-keeled she would always take my mother's side. So, my suspicions would align her against me. I just let it go, for now.

"Mom said that she wants you to go down to Spencer's Funeral Home and make all the arrangements. You need me to go with you?"

I chuckled. "She's being optimistic. I heard her suggest that to J.C., but I didn't agree to do it. What do I know about that kind of stuff? Besides, she's the widow. It's her responsibility to take care of this. Why is she shoving it off on me?"

"I guess she's a bit upset. And you know Mama, she's..."

"Yes, she's the iron lady. She's cold and hard. It wouldn't kill her to show a little emotion every now and then."

Denise stood up and frowned. "Look, I know that you're hurting. But you should go a little easier on Mama. She loves you unconditionally and you should reciprocate that love."

"I don't doubt that, Denise. And I love her with all my heart as well. But she's still a tough, emotionless woman. You can't deny that."

"She is who she is. I accept her faults and all," Denise said.

I was upsetting Denise and it just wasn't the time to get on her bad side.

"Look, I'm sorry. I'm just a little rattled right now so please forgive me."

"It's okay. Anyway, Mama asked if you would come to the kitchen. Everyone is in there and we need to talk about the arrangements and what we're going to do about Laura's graduation."

"Sounds like fun," I said, jumped off the picnic table and followed Denise into the house.

***

When I walked into the kitchen with Denise, everyone – except for Dickie and Laura - was huddled around the table. Tanya was in the living room watching television, which was one of the few times she refrained from sticking her ears into an adult conversation. J.C. had already left.

"Well there he is," Stephanie moaned. She was still dressed in her pajamas, and her hair was dancing all over her head.

"It's not like I ran away. I was just out back."

"Well, we've been waiting for you," My mother started. "We need to talk about everything that's happened and the plans for the next two days."

Then I spoke, without thinking. "It's simple. Harry killed himself, you want me to go make all the arrangements, and you're probably still thinking about going to the graduation. Should we wait for you to return or should we plant him in the ground without..."

My mother had heard enough. She caught me on the cheek with her right hand. "I'm still your mother, Robert, and you won't speak to me like that."

I deserved the slap. While I was being flippant about the entire situation, I really had no idea what my mother was going through. My problem was that I didn't see any overt sadness or grief from her. Perhaps she was actually grieving, and this was just her way of dealing with it.

"I'm sorry, Mom," I apologized and rubbed my chin. I looked over at Stephanie, who had a huge grin on her face, and I said, "I'm glad you are amused by this."

My mother ignored my comment. "You sister graduates tomorrow, June

10th. We'll need to have the funeral on Monday, to give Harry's relatives a chance to get here. Denise, you and Bobby need to stay here while Stephanie and I attend the graduation. We'll be back late tomorrow night or Saturday morning, and we'll bring Laura back with us. Douglas, you need to find Richard. He needs to know what has happened."

"Damn," Doug moaned. He clearly didn't want to be the designated 'Dickie Tracker'.

My mother turned to me. "Did Dickie tell you where he was going?"

"No, he didn't say," I answered. Dickie was on the run from something, and I doubted if anyone would locate him any time soon. Dickie would show up when he was ready to be found. For all I knew, he could be in Canada.

Mom turned to Doug and said, "In that case, start with some of his friends and call his workplace in Chicago. Maybe he went back home."

Doug looked at me and rolled his eyes. I laughed.

"This isn't funny, boys," my mother said.

"Bobby," she continued, "After you finish at Spencer's, I need you to go down to see Tom Zigelhofer and get everything straight. Have him give you a copy of the will."

"Mama I don't want to see his will," I complained. She had pushed the funeral arrangements off on me, and now she wanted me to take care of the legal matters. It didn't seem fair that I had to deal with both the mortician and a lawyer.

"Don't worry. He left everything to me, so there are no surprises. He had left a few things to his sister and niece in Atlanta, but I had him revise the will six months ago. Just pick up the copy and bring it here. Also find out from Zigelhofer the legal process. We don't want to start giving things away without knowing if it is proper or not."

"Mama," Stephanie interrupted, "Can I have the green Chrysler?"

"Yes. As soon as I locate the title, and Zigelhofer says that it's okay, I'll sign it over to you."

I couldn't believe that Stephanie actually brought the subject up at such an inappropriate time. Her greed had no bounds. I guessed she felt she

49

needed to put her request in while still sober.

"So are you taking the Malibu or the Chrysler to Columbus?" I asked.

"Why? Mama gave the car to me; you heard her," Stephanie snapped.

"Look, I don't want the car. I need to know what you are driving because if I'm going to run these errands, I'll need one of the cars to get around in."

My mother handed me the keys to the Malibu. "We'll take the Chrysler to Columbus. It's roomier than the Malibu." I took the keys from her and she continued with, "Okay, I am going to pack. Bobby, you get going now so that we can get all these things cleared up. Here," she said, and handed me a white envelope.

"What's this?" I asked.

"That's the money for Spencer's. If he needs more, just take my bank book with you, and stop by the bank and withdraw it. You're a signer on the account, so it shouldn't be a problem. And listen; be smart about your choices. He doesn't need to go to heaven in a gilded chariot. Any economical box will be okay."

Okay, pretty col, I thought. But I wasn't going to argue with her. I took the envelope from her and waited while she went to get her bank book. When she returned, I simply grabbed it without comment and headed for the door.

"Wait up," Denise said. "I'll come with you."

***

Things went fairly smoothly at Spencer's Funeral Home. I didn't have much work to do because J.C. had pulled some choices together, and Denise made most of the decisions. Once we had chosen the coffin, we worked through all the administrative details – day of service, Wake – those sorts of things, along with the suit in which he would be buried.

Satisfied that all the details were taken care of, I discussed the cost for everything with J.C. He asked me how much money I had in the envelope, and I told him. Coincidentally, that was the exact amount of the entire funeral. I got a receipt and Denise and I left.

"God, I'm glad that's over," I said to Denise when we climbed into the car. "You want me to drop you off at the house or do you want to go to Zigelhofer's with me?"

"I'll just go to the lawyer's with you. It shouldn't take too long."

Tom Zigelhofer had been my mother's lawyer since he graduated from law school. Before him, his father, Zach, had been our family's attorney, but he died shortly after Tom had graduated. Everyone in the Zigelhofer family had become lawyers – Tom, his older brother Zachary Junior, his sister Victoria and his younger brother Carlton. I always felt that Tom was the slow one of the bunch. It took him three attempts to pass the state bar, and when he finally did, according to the rumors, he had a little help.

He had a small family practice in the downtown area, so after we left Spencer's we didn't have far to drive. Tom mainly kept his practice to probate matters – wills, estates, trusts, etc. So he was fairly competent in those areas. But, I wouldn't have trusted him in a court as a trial lawyer.

I parked in front of the building where his office was located. It was an old, turn-of-the- century, red-brick, four-story building. The few tenants that remained in the old structure were on the first floor. Zigelhofer's office was an old store front. To the right of the entry way was a huge window with Zigelhofer's name stenciled in black. When I looked through the window, I could see him seated behind his desk.

The office was a mess. Legal tomes were scattered everywhere. And it was hot. "You need to get an air-conditioner," I suggested, walking into his office.

He smiled and got up from his desk. "I have one," he said and laughed as he pointed to a small, cheap oscillating fan sitting atop a file cabinet.

"Yeah, that'll do the job," I joked.

"Bobby, how are you?" he said and shook my hand. "And, Denise, I haven't seen you in years. First of all, I want to offer my deepest sympathies. Harry was a wonderful man, and I was sorry to hear of his passing."

"Thanks, Tom," I said, and sat down in one of the chairs across from his desk. Denise sat next to me. "We appreciate your kind words. Harry liked you, as well. He once told me that the best decision he made was to leave

Prentiss and come over to you."

"Well, I appreciate that because you know Prentiss is a well-known name in this city. That means a lot to me."

"Tom, my mother asked me to come down and get a copy of Harry's will," I explained.

Tom frowned. "Well, I can't simply give it to her."

"Why not?" I asked.

"Harry never discussed his will with you, Bobby?" Zigelhofer asked.

I could see that he was a bit confused. "Why would he discuss the will with me? This was between you, Harry and my mother."

Tom sat down across from Denise and me. He paused for a minute and then shuffled some papers. "Your mom is no longer in Harry's will."

Denise almost fell out of her chair. "What do you mean she's not in the will? She's his wife," Denise barked. "She has to be in the will."

Tom cleared his throat. "Harry made some changes. He said that this was a marriage of convenience, and that Mrs. Bremen had her own assets – houses, savings and other property. He felt she would have no need for any additional assets, because she was financially stable and capable of taking care of herself without his assets."

"Wait a minute," Denise protested. "My mother came in with Harry just six months ago and made this change. She should get everything."

"Well, unfortunately, Denise, Harry came in last Tuesday and updated his will. I asked him then if he wanted to include Mrs. Bremen in the will, and he said "no". I tried to convince him otherwise, but he insisted his mind was made up. I've already probated the will with the courts."

"Well, okay," I started. "You know my mother is going to be pissed, but if he changed it, he changed it. What should I tell her?"

"I don't know, but I'm glad that you came in, Bobby. I have some paperwork for you to sign. Please read this and sign at the bottom," he said and startled me by pushing a brown envelope and a pen across the desk toward me.

I opened it. It was Harry's last will and testament along with some legal papers. I quickly scanned through it. "Oh, shit," I said and sat the paperwork on the desk.

"What's wrong?" Denise asked.

"He left everything to Bobby," Tom started. "The house, two savings accounts, his personal checking, the two cars, and a rental property in Atlanta, Georgia."

"All of it?" Denise asked.

"Yes, all of it," Tom answered.

I was speechless. I didn't have time to process my apparent financial windfall. I thought only of my mother and how pissed she was going to be.

"Tom, I can't afford this. I don't have a job to pay mortgages and car notes," I said.

"It's all paid off. The cars and the houses have clear titles. They're all yours once everything clears probate. You can do whatever you want with them."

"Do you have any idea why he would do this?" I asked.

"I have no idea. I asked him to reconsider, but he told me his mind was made up. Everything goes to you. I'll hold on to the titles until you have your records in order, but if you need them before that they'll be here in my safe. As for the cash, it's yours. There are no debts – Harry paid off everyone, so probate won't be a problem. Once everything clears, as the executor of Harry's estate, I'll make sure his wishes are carried out and the proper documentation is filed with the courts. Go by the First National Bank when you get a chance. All three accounts are there. You'll need to sign some paperwork. The bank manager will be expecting you. Since Harry made you a co-owner on his bank accounts, probate is not a concern."

"So that's it?" I asked, still a bit stunned from the revelation.

"Well, yes, but you have to sign the paperwork I gave you first," he smiled and pointed to where my signature was needed. I quickly signed and gave the papers back to him.

"Okay, Bobby, we're all finished here. When you have all the funeral arrangements in place, have the bills sent to me, and I will make sure everything is taken care of."

"We've already paid Spencer," I said.

"Don't worry. I'll deal with Spencer. I suspect he overcharged you. That's his way. When someone dies, he shows up and gets everyone in a panic and then takes advantage of the situation. I assume your mother gave you the money for the funeral, so I'll make sure she is reimbursed. And believe me, when I am through with Spencer, he'll give you a discount."

"Thanks, Tom," I said, and started for the door. Denise was already outside standing by the car.

"Remember, Bobby, if you need anything, let me know," he reminded, shook my hand and opened the door for me.

I walked over to the car and unlocked the passenger door for Denise. Before she got in the car she looked over at me and said, "Mom isn't going to take this well."

***

I had hoped that when Denise and I returned to the house, our mother would have already left for the graduation. But when we pulled in front, the Chrysler was sitting in the driveway. It was nearly three in the afternoon, and I was disappointed to see the car still there. This wasn't going to be easy.

Instead of parking behind the green Chrysler, I parked the Malibu onto the front lawn. When Harry and my mother had entertained, they often allowed people to park on the grass.

Denise looked over at me and said, "Good luck, rich man," and laughed. She hadn't said much to me in the car. In fact, she never mentioned a thing about the money. I was glad because I had my own problems to deal with, and anything she might have said would have only compounded my difficulties.

"You mean soon to be dead man?" I joked.

We walked into the house. Doug was sitting on the couch, with the telephone pressed to his ear. I assumed he hadn't located Dickie yet. He nodded to me just as my mother came out of the bedroom.

My mother, a short, stocky woman, was carrying a suitcase nearly as tall as she. "Did you get everything straight with Spencer and the lawyer?" she asked.

"Yes ma'am, we did," I said and glanced over to Denise, who quickly hurried around me into the kitchen. *Coward*, I thought, as she disappeared.

"Well, just leave the receipt from Spencer on the table. And give me the copy of the will. I'll look it over on the drive to Columbus."

"I don't have a copy of the will, Mama," I said, a bit nervous and hesitant to relay the entire story to her.

"Why not, Bobby? I asked you to get the copy."

"Tom wouldn't give me a copy for you," I explained, and stood back to ready myself for the impending Sarah Foster-Bremen explosion.

"Why wouldn't he give you a copy? I'm Harry's wife. I have a right to a copy of his will."

"Yes, you do. But to get a copy you are going to need to go down to his office."

"Wait a minute," she started and sat the suitcase to the side. "Come sit down and walk me through this," she said and took a seat at the kitchen table. "You and Denise were to go to the lawyer and get a copy of Harry's will for me. Now you are telling me that I can't have a copy. This makes no sense."

"Well, Mama," Denise started somewhat gingerly, "I guess you should know. We couldn't get you a copy of the will because Harry didn't leave you anything."

"Don't play with me, girl," my mother snapped.

"It's true, Mom. Harry didn't leave anything to you," I confirmed.

"He didn't leave me a dime?"

"No, ma'am. Nothing," I said. I wanted to delay this as long as possible.

"Well if he didn't leave it to me, do you have any idea who he left everything to? Was it that whore sister and niece of his in Atlanta, Georgia?" she yelled, and stood up from the table.

"No, they didn't get anything, either," I said, just as Stephanie walked into the kitchen. Moments later, Doug joined us.

"No word on Dickie," he said, giving me a brief break from the hell that was sure to soon come my way.

"No one has seen him?" she asked.

"Nope, no one has seen him in two days. In fact, we were the last to see him. There's no telling where he is. I guess we're going to have to hope he calls."

"Keep looking for him," she snapped and then turned back to me.

"Now, do you have any idea who Harry left his things to?" She reiterated. "We just changed the damn will six months ago. When did he change it back? Did Zigelhofer tell you?"

"Yes, ma'am. He changed his will last week," I nervously offered. I wasn't scared of my mother. I worried about of her reaction, though. She could go over the top and into an attack mode at any moment. Her attacks mostly were hurtful verbal barrages of hate and meanness. Sometimes though, she would strike out in anger. And this worried me, because I didn't know what I would do if she came at me in that manner.

"Then whom did he leave it to?" she persisted.

I paused for a few seconds to word it properly. But my silence only made things more uncomfortable for us all, so I simply blurted it out. "He left everything to me."

My mother was quiet for a moment and then quickly angered. "I can't believe you. Here this man has killed himself, and you would take advantage of this situation by telling a sick joke like this. Bobby, this isn't funny. Now, tell me who gets his property."

"It's true, Mama," Denise intervened. "Bobby is telling the truth. Harry left everything to him. I saw the will. Everything has been signed over to Bobby."

My mother's jaw almost hit the floor. "This isn't a joke?" she asked, nearly whispering.

The news shocked everyone in the room into silence. Then Stephanie began to cry. Doug just turned and walked out the room.

"No, Mama, it's not a joke. Harry left everything to me. Apparently, he told Tom that you brought your own assets into the marriage, and had more than enough to take care of yourself should something happen to him."

"Well, good for you then," she said and without another word stormed from the kitchen to the bedroom and closed the door.

"What have you done?" Stephanie screamed. "How did you pull off this con?"

I really didn't want to deal with Stephanie. "Look, I didn't do anything. Harry called me and asked me to come home to drive him and Mama to Laura's graduation. I just showed up; that's all I did. I've never asked Harry for anything."

"Somehow you got Harry to cut Mama out of his will," she accused and went back to the bedroom to join Mom. There was no telling what these two were going to conjure while they were back there.

"Don't worry about it, man," Doug said as he walked back into the room. "Let's just wait for things to calm down, and I'm sure something can be worked out to make everyone happy."

"It's already worked out," Denise said. "Harry left it all to Bobby. There's nothing else to work out."

I sensed at that point, Denise was beginning to turn on me.

In a way, my mother's surprise was a bit hypocritical because I knew for a fact that had Harry been the longest survivor, he would not have inherited anything from her. She would have left everything to her children – well, to Stephanie and Dickie anyway.

What no one knew at that point was that I wanted nothing to do with the inheritance – maybe a little of the money to pay off my college, but other than that, the houses, cars, and remaining money my mother could keep. However, this greed that had infected our family was a bit unseemly. So before I informed anyone of my intentions, I decided that I would wait it out and get through the funeral, so that things could settle down. My head needed to be cleared, and my grief lessened before I could make any of these decisions.

All that changed when the bedroom door opened and my mother thundered down the hall. She walked into the kitchen and said, "Sign it over to me. Today."

***

Her request caught me by surprise. In fact, I was stunned that she would even suggest it. But when I looked into her eyes, I knew my mother was very serious. "What do you mean, Mama?" I asked.

"You're not stupid, Bobby. I was very clear. It's four o'clock. We have plenty of time to get down to Zigelhofer's office and have you sign Harry's estate over to me."

"I'm not following this. What brought this on?"

"It's mine, Bobby. It's all rightfully mine. He owed this to me, and I mean to have it. I'm not going to let you or any of the children stand in my way. This belongs to me. So get the keys to the car and take me down to the lawyer's office, and we can get this settled today."

"Mama, there's no rush. We can get all these matters taken care of after the funeral."

"We'll do it today, do you understand me?" she screamed. When my mother's face turned red, I knew that absolute hell was not far off. Her anger would be followed by an ongoing barrage of verbal assaults, which often culminated in a little of mild violence.

"Come on, Mama, please, let this go for now," I pleaded. There was no way that I would, under any type of duress, relinquish control of Harry's estate. I viewed the entire topic - in light of the circumstances - inappropriate and my mother's demands over the top.

"I won't let it go," she screamed and slapped me as hard as she could across the face. "You stole this from me. Somehow, Bobby," she screamed and slapped me again. "You stole this all from me."

I had seen my mother angry before but never like this. My face stung. I rubbed my chin and remained steady. I asked, "Mama, why would you say that?"

"You were always kissing up to Harry. Why did he give it all to you, Bobby? What did you do to persuade him to take it away from me? How could you betray me?"

"Mama, how could you believe I would do this? I didn't..."

58

"You, bastard, you stole this from me. And I demand you get your ass in the car and go to the lawyer's and make this right."

She reached up to hit me again, but this time, I grabbed her arm. Doug jumped up from the chair and began to lunge toward me, but I immediately backed him down. "Doug, sit your ass down," I said to him. "You know I won't hurt Mama, but you also know I'm not going to let her hit me again. I haven't done anything."

My mother pushed away from me. "You need to tell me if you are going to go downtown and make this right."

"No, ma'am. I don't think I want to do that," I said.

"Then you're not welcome here," she snapped. "Get your things and get out of my house."

"Okay, I'll do that," I said, and started toward the basement to pack my duffel.

Denise stood up from the table. "Mama, you need to cool down. First of all, this is Bobby's house, now. His name is on the deed. The two cars out there belong to Bobby. It's all his. You can't just throw him out. Secondly, this is your son. He was raised by you. He is a fair, decent human being. What you're doing is wrong."

"Leave Mama alone," Stephanie intervened. "Why are you ganging up on her? The house, cars and money belong to her, and now you're both conspiring to steal it."

"Quiet, Stephanie. They're right," my mother said, miraculously cooling down. "I was out of line. My anger got the best of me. Let's get through the funeral, and we will revisit this afterwards." She turned to me. "Bobby, I hope you can forgive me. I was upset and said some things that I shouldn't have said. And I'm sorry for hitting you," she apologized.

"It's okay, Mama. We'll talk about this after the funeral." This was my mother's normal strategy – calm down, apologize, give me a couple of days to get my mind right, and then get exactly what she wanted. However, inside I was furious. I loved my mother, but some things and actions were difficult to let go. Today, she crossed the line. And while I would forgive her in words, I wasn't sure I would ever be able to forgive her in my heart.

My mother turned to Stephanie and said, "If you still feel up to driving - and if it's okay with Bobby - why don't we take the green car and go to your sister's graduation. We'll be back tomorrow night or Saturday morning."

I saw how the tone was going to be between the two of us until this situation was resolved. "Yes, it's okay with me. Take whichever car you want."

"Thank you, your highness," Stephanie said with a mocking curtsy.

Before I could respond, she turned to Tanya, "Get your things in the car, girl. We're going to see your aunt Laura graduate from college. Something your uncle Bobby will probably never do."

I ignored her digs. I took my mother's suitcase and put it in the trunk of the Chrysler. Doug followed with Tanya and Stephanie's bags.

"That was quite a scene in there," he said as he put the bags in the car.

"Well, it got a little out of hand."

"Can you blame her for being angry?" Doug asked.

"I understand her being upset. What I don't understand is why she attacked me. I had nothing to do with Harry's decision. I had nothing to do with his death."

"Well I'm not quite sure about that."

"I didn't have anything to do with him leaving the property to me. Why would you even think that?" I asked angrily.

"I believe you, Bobby. I don't think you manipulated the inheritance," he said.

"You fucker, how the hell can you believe that I had anything to do with his death?"

Doug grinned. "Let's just say I have been asking some questions today. And you don't come out squeaky clean in this."

"Harry killed himself. How could you possibly think I had anything to do with that?" I asked. I couldn't believe that he would actually lay an accusation like that on me.

"I have my reasons. And I'm not saying another word about it until Mama is on the road."

"You actually believe I played a role in Harry's suicide," I said to him as he walked back toward the house.

"I don't believe it. I'm sure of it," Doug said and disappeared into the house.

***

I pretty much ignored Doug for the first hour after our mother had left. I wanted to beat the shit out of him. The accusation he leveled against me was beyond absurd. I had nothing to do with Harry killing himself, and was puzzled as to how he could come to believe such a thing. But instead of resorting to violence, I simply chose to ignore him.

My family's antics, thus far, awoke me to a sobering reality. I was stunned that my mother could act with such outright greed. I was equally stunned that my brother believed that I played a role in Harry's tragic death. I loved Harry Bremen, as though he had been my very own father. I wouldn't have done anything to hurt him or assist him in hurting himself.

I was sitting on the couch relaxing when Denise came from the basement and sat in the chair across from me.

"Doug was downstairs with me, and he's talking some craziness that you had something to do with Harry's death," she said.

"If you believe that, then you're crazier than Doug," I answered.

"He says he has evidence," she persisted.

"I don't know what kind of evidence he has. I had nothing to do with Harry putting a gun to his head and blowing his brains out. I wasn't in the room with him. I was out here with everyone else when it happened."

"Well, he is pretty insistent. He told me that he would be up here in a minute or two to confront you."

"I'm not worried about Doug. Don't believe his bullshit, Denise. I wouldn't hurt Harry."

"Yes you would," Doug said as he walked through the kitchen to the living room. "You may not have done it intentionally, but you did hurt him. I think you knew exactly what you were doing."

"What the fuck are you talking about, man?" I asked.

At that moment, the doorbell rang. "That's why I'm here," a voice boomed through the screen door from outside.

It was Dickie. I should have known he would turn up now that there was an upside for him. He came inside and walked across the room toward me.

"Doug tells me that our little brother has been busy. He says you might as well have put the gun to Harry's head and pulled the trigger."

"Doug's out of his mind," I said.

"Am I, Bobby?" Doug asked. "While you were out laying claim to your small fortune today, I put two and two together and came to an interesting conclusion that you all might want to hear."

"I'd sure like to hear it," Dickie bellowed and sat on the couch and gave me a playful hug. "Don't you want to hear it, killer?" he teased.

"I don't believe you two. How can you even think such a thing?"

"I'll tell you how," Doug interjected. "I heard that on Wednesday night, Jimmy came by looking for his girlfriend. She was downstairs with you. Apparently," he said, and looked at Denise, "Harry went crazy and pulled a gun on Jimmy."

"That's right. We talked him down," I explained.

"Talked him down? I heard that Mama grabbed the gun from Harry."

"She did. But we still had to talk him down."

"So here's the interesting part, Dickie," Doug said, then turned to me and asked, "What happened to the gun Harry pulled on Jimmy?"

"Mom grabbed it from him," I started.

"What did she do with it?" Doug persisted.

"She gave it to me. So what?" Then it occurred to me where this was going. "It wasn't the same gun, Doug. It was a .25 Caliber Colt that he pulled on Jimmy."

"So, what you're saying is the gun that Mama took from Harry and gave to you was not the same gun with which Harry used to shoot himself?"

"That's right," I answered.

"Okay. Prove it. Show us the gun that Mama took from Harry," Doug requested.

"I don't have it," I said. It was hard to believe that my own brother would accuse me.

"Why don't you have it?" Denise asked.

"Because I gave it back to Harry," I said. "He took it in the room with him."

"Well little brother," Dickie barked, "I think Doug may be on to something. While you might not have pulled the trigger you did give Harry the means."

"He killed himself with a Baretta. He pulled a small Colt .25 caliber on Jimmy. They were different guns."

"Then why didn't we find a Colt in his room? We've searched the bedroom top to bottom, and no other gun was found. I think the only gun he owned was the one he killed himself with," Doug said, "and you gave him the means when you handed it back to him that night."

"You're crazy," I said. I knew my weapons from my Army days. And I knew these were completely different guns. I could tell a Colt from a Baretta. And Harry definitely pulled a Colt on Jimmy.

"I think you're the crazy one. And quite frankly, Bobby, I think you knew that Harry was unstable and that's why you gave the gun back to him," Doug accused.

"You have to admit it wasn't a responsible thing to do," Denise chimed in.

"Denise, it wasn't the same gun. I'm telling all three of you – who have not spent one day in the military – that I know my weapons. And these were two different guns."

"Yeah, right. You better hope Mama doesn't find out. I think she could probably take this information to courts and have this whole inheritance thing overturned," Doug said.

"Look, I don't care what you do. I had nothing to do with Harry's death. So tell her what you want."

"You don't want that, Bobby," Dickie said. "You see; we need to keep Mama happy. If she believes that one of her sons had something to do with her husband's death, well, that won't be good. And even if, through some miracle, you come out clean in this, we still will have planted the seeds of doubt in her mind."

"Denise, are you buying this shit?" I asked angrily and got up from my seat and headed for the door.

"Sit down, Bobby, and hear them out," she insisted.

"I get it. This is a classic shakedown. All three of you are involved. So what's the upside for you?"

"Okay, little brother, here's how we play this. We don't tell the authorities or Mama anything. You sign the house over to her. Then give the green Chrysler to Stephanie. Sell the house in Georgia and add the proceeds to the three bank accounts. You split the money six ways, each of us getting an equal share. You can deduct the value of the green car from Stephanie's cut. You take the Malibu and everyone is happy," Denise proposed.

"So that's the deal, huh?" I asked. "My own brothers and sister are trying to blackmail me."

"It's a fair division, Bobby," Doug insisted. "You need to consider this."

It surprised me that the Colt had conveniently disappeared. But more surprising were my sibling's accusations. They were looking for an easy payday.

My initial plans had been to split the estate among my brothers and sisters. I didn't even want the car. However, their accusations were a game changer for me. Now that they had allowed their greed to get out in front of the truth, I decided to leave them out, altogether.

"So, that's the deal. No negotiation?" I asked.

"None," Dickie said.

"Well, give me a couple of days to mull it over," I requested.

"Okay, we'll give you until Sunday night. You need to let us know your decision then. Or else we go to Mama," Doug threatened.

"It warms my heart to find out that I have such loving brothers and sisters," I said sarcastically, got up from the couch and walked to the front door.

I stepped out in the evening air. It was getting late now, and the sun was setting on another day. Harry had been gone for a little over twenty four hours, but it seemed so much longer. I wished that I could go back two days and prevent this entire episode. More than anything, I wished that I could just sit down and talk to Harry.

I sat on the front porch and rested as the night comfortably settled in around me. Before long, it was totally dark outside and starting to get a little chilly. I went inside and fell asleep on the couch.

DAY 4 – FRIDAY

The doorbell rang – it was habitual now, and no one in my family would take the initiative to answer the damn thing. That was my new role, I guessed, to be the doorman for the family.

When Harry had installed the new bell a year earlier, he opted to go with a single loud ring versus a full stanza of "God Save the Queen". Thank God for small miracles.

I pulled myself up, dropped my feet to the floor, checked my mid-section to make sure I was presentable and walked over to the front door. When I opened it, I saw five complete strangers standing on the porch, staring at me.

I rubbed my eyes. "Can I help you?" I asked.

The person in front, a short, stocky woman who looked to be in her fifties or sixties spoke up. "Hello, I am Eleanor Bremen-Thurman. Harry was my brother."

"Good morning," I greeted. "Please come in," I invited and stepped aside while Eleanor and her entourage of four entered the house. When they had crowded into the living room, I cleared the couch and offered them a seat.

"I'm sorry. The past few days have been upsetting. I'm Robert Foster, Harry's stepson," I introduced.

"It's nice to meet you, Robert," Eleanor said to me, very politely. But I detected a small bit of aloofness in her voice. "This is my daughter, Chandra, my husband, Herbert, and my son, Phillip. And the quiet man over there is my brother – and of course, Harry's brother - Paul."

I stepped toward them and shook everyone's hand as they crowded onto the sofa and love seat. Eleanor wore little, if any makeup. Her hair, with noticeable streaks of gray, fell onto her shoulders. I sensed that she was the unquestionable leader of her family from the way she led the conversation and directed everyone around. But just as evident was everyone's response to her. When she spoke, they listened. When she ordered, they obeyed. So, she at least had that in common with my mother.

Her daughter, Chandra, immediately caught my eye. Thin – but shapely - I looked at her attractive face and quickly contrasted it with her mother and father and wondered from which parent had she inherited her beauty. She didn't seem to have either's likeness so apparently, I thought, there was a milk man somewhere in Georgia the spitting image of her. Chandra seemed bright, and the smile on her faced hinted to an enthusiasm that I hoped to experience over the coming days.

Her brother Phillip seemed to be the opposite of Chandra. He entered the house quietly and kept his eyes fixed on the floor. He came across as withdrawn and shy. And unlike Chandra, he looked exactly like his mother.

When I spoke to him, he barely acknowledged my greeting, avoided eye contact and managed only a slight grin then quickly turned his attention back toward the floor.

Chandra and Phillip's father, Herbert, also came across as a quiet person, even though Eleanor had mentioned her brother Paul as being the quiet one.

Herbert looked around the living room, as though he was casing the house out. He didn't say a word to me, and deferred a handshake. His eyes though, belied his soft demeanor. This was a man who had been defeated in his life. He could easily join Harry any day through stroke or heart attack, or even by his own hand. So maybe his quietness stemmed from the fact that he had been whipped.

Harry's brother, Paul, was a puzzling case. The spitting image of Harry, sans the glasses, it was as though Harry had never left. However, Paul's mannerisms, thus far, were a bit strange. When he tried to speak, before he could get a word out, Eleanor glared at him, and he immediately clamped his thoughts. During our brief, "get to know you" conversation he just nodded and smiled politely. He never spoke a word. In fact, the only two people in the room that said more than a full sentence were Eleanor and Chandra.

I chuckled inside. While my mother was a ball buster in all ways that I could determine, my brothers and I maintained our independent spirits and hot-heads. In fact, though we often lost, we would still go toe-to-toe with our mom on a variety of issues. These men in my presence were whipped – thoroughly whipped and beat down by the dominance of the females in their family. The next few days were going to be very interesting.

I continued my pleasantries and said, "It's nice to meet you all. Please accept my condolences. I cared deeply for Harry, and I'm saddened that he is no longer with us."

"Yes, it was a shock. As soon as your mother called we were on the road. We loved our brother very much," Eleanor said.

"My mother is out of town at the moment. She will be back tonight..."

"Her husband is dead, and she is out of town?" Eleanor interrupted. Based on her sour look and tone, I figured this was going to be an old-fashioned shoot-out between this lady and my mother.

Eleanor's daughter, Chandra, picked up on the jab. She lifted her head and glanced disapprovingly at her mother. The two of them had an agenda, I surmised, as I watched them glance furtively back and forth at each other. I didn't know what they were after but I was prepared to protect my family's interest.

Granted, my mother and I didn't end the day on a positive note. And of course, my sibling's lame attempt at a bribe pissed me off. But, they were my blood, so I felt obliged to put up with all of their shenanigans, no matter how stupid or misguided.

And despite what happened between us privately, I would never betray them or align myself against them. So, anything that Eleanor might posit in the days to come wouldn't be embraced by Bobby Foster. I would deal with my family in my own way. And now, I assumed, I was going to have to find a way to deal with Eleanor and hers.

If my mother had heard how Eleanor retorted, she would have probably stood up, walked over to Eleanor and told her to go fuck herself. But fortunately, even though I knew how my mother would treat Eleanor's slight, she had also raised me to be polite and well-mannered towards my elders. My interactions with this family had to be delicate and diplomatic until Sarah Foster-Bremen returned.

"This all happened so suddenly, and it absolutely crushed my mother," I offered and continued, "She and Harry had planned to go see my sister graduate from the University today, something he indicated he was looking forward to doing. Out of respect for his memory she decided to go."

"Yes, I guess I understand," Eleanor said. I had been around people like Eleanor many times before, and of course, she did not understand. If something was contrary to her agenda there was no way she would try to understand it.

But in that regard, I was like my mother and didn't give a fuck if she understood or not. I didn't think anything else about it and turned my thoughts to my next move.

I wondered where my brothers and sisters were. Maybe they had a "come to Jesus" meeting this morning and were waiting for the right time to sit down with me and apologize. I could have used their help in entertaining our guests.

Or possibly they already knew who was here and decided to keep a low profile. Eleanor and my mother had a history of bad blood between them. For some reason, Mom didn't like either Eleanor or Chandra. Apparently, it all went bad at a Bremen Reunion in Atlanta the previous summer. Mom never gave me all the details, but I knew there was no love lost between them. Maybe that was why my sister and brothers had initially allowed me to suffer our visitors alone.

Of course, just when I thought I had been deserted, Dickie emerged from the basement wearing only gym shorts and white athletic socks.

While he got an "oh my God," gasp from Eleanor and one of her "holier than thou" looks, Dickie's chiseled frame immediately caught Chandra's attention. I knew then, that whatever slight chance I had with her, might have departed as soon as her eyes fell on Dickie's abs. Although there were a few years between them, Dickie's youthful appearance would easily compensate for that. He had hooked Chandra.

Of course, my mother had called both Chandra and Eleanor whores, so she must have known something. I was sure though, that before they returned to Atlanta, either Dickie or I would validate if Chandra was a whore or not.

"Well hello, ladies," Dickie started, then said, "Oh, please excuse me. I didn't think anyone was up here. I apologize," he said, then turned to the three men in the room and said, "Gentlemen."

He ran back down the stairs.

"That was my brother, Dickie. He'll be back in a minute," I said.

Denise opened the guest bedroom door. I thanked God that she was fully dressed. She came down the hall and joined us.

"So, this is Eleanor, I presume," she started and walked over to her. "I'm Denise. My mother has told me so much about you and your lovely family," she turned and introduced herself to Chandra, Phillip, Herbert Thurman and Paul Bremen.

"It's so nice to meet you, Denise," Eleanor started. "When we heard the news we came right away. Paul and I were very close to Harry."

Yeah right, I said to myself. They were so close that Harry rarely mentioned them. When he did – at least the one time he did to me – he complained about how money hungry they were. I believed that he referred to his sister Eleanor as a user. So it didn't surprise me that they had arrived so soon after his death. We had expected them for the wake and interment on Monday morning, but here they were before the weekend, sitting with us.

I had come to notice, in my short twenty-five years on the earth, that after someone passed away, the twenty-four hours immediately following their death is known to me as the "looting" hours. That is when distant relatives unexpectedly converge upon the deceased's property and begin to take anything that isn't nailed down. I was sure that this was Eleanor's intent, but she must have been disappointed to pull up and find the house, full of people. Her window of opportunity had closed.

"Well, it has been a long trip, and if it's okay with you, I think we need to freshen up," Eleanor said.

"Okay, well, we will be here all day, so when you are rested, you are welcome to come back over-"

"Oh, this is embarrassing," Eleanor started, "It seems that all the hotels in town are booked, so we were hoping we could stay here until the funeral."

I knew right away that they were freeloaders. It was June 10th and there was nothing going on in our small town that would book all the hotels solid. But I didn't embarrass them and simply said, "Well, I'm sure we can make room for everyone."

"Thank you very much, Bobby," Eleanor said and turned to the men, "Will you three get the bags out the car?"

Phillip, Herbert and Paul obediently walked outside. She turned back to me. "After we are rested, I would like to discuss a few financial matters with you and your family regarding Harry's estate," she smiled.

"Well, my mother may be back tonight, and I think that will be an appropriate time to talk about anything regarding Harry's affairs."

"Of course. In the meantime, I would like to get the name of Harry's lawyer, if that is not too much to ask. We have some joint property together, and I would like to make sure all the paperwork is in order."

"Yes, that isn't a problem. His name is Tom Zigelhofer, and he has an office downtown. You may want to catch him early though, because I believe on Fridays he leaves at noon," I explained. *Boy, is she going to get a surprise when she visits Tom,* I thought.

I concluded that everyone around me was going to be pissed at me before all was said and done. So far, I had managed to piss off my mother, brothers and sisters. Now, the Thurman family and Harry's brother were on deck.

While they were getting their bags, I ran for the bathroom. Harry had always wanted to put a shower in the basement but never got around to it. With this line, I would have to wait too long for the shower, so I needed to jump ahead. I had things to do this morning. I had a gun to find.

***

When I left the house, they were lined up waiting for the shower. Eleanor caught me at the door to get directions to the lawyer's office. She was also a bit curious as to where I was going, but it was none of her business.

I was damn near certain that Harry had accosted Jimmy with a small Colt pistol. It was a lady's gun, as far as I was concerned. It was an automatic pistol, small enough to fit in the palm of one's hand, but it wasn't very effective. If fired properly, it could kill a person, but more than likely, a hit to the torso would result in a hospital visit, but probably not death. Of course, point-blank, it was lethal.

I knew weapons pretty well. I had spent some time in the Army as a Military Policeman, so not only did I use a variety of firearms, but I also confiscated them. So there weren't many handguns that I couldn't identify. Harry had drawn a Colt. I was sure of this. And the gun that lay next to Harry's body – the one that he used to kill himself - was definitely a Baretta.

All of this really seemed to be much ado about nothing. But this threat, as weak as it may have been, could gain momentum and believability from the gullible people around me. So I needed to find this small handgun as evidence that I had nothing to do with an assisted suicide. I thought maybe Doug had somehow hidden the gun when he cleaned the blood off the floor.

I figured if I could run Jimmy down and talk to him, he might be able to help me clear this up. My friend Jimmy was a thug. And being such, he was adept with weapons as well and would have known what kind of gun was pulled on him.

I wasn't sure where Jimmy was staying, so I thought I would start my search at Vivian's place. When I had dated Vivian, she stayed with her mother, father and older sister on one of the main thorough fares in my home town.

Before going there though, I needed to stop by the bank, sign off on the paperwork and withdraw some money. I figured that any information that I would ultimately get from Jimmy might come at a cost.

The First National Bank was in the middle of town, on the main road that ran east and west through the downtown area. I found a convenient parking space directly in front of the bank. I entered, walked past the guard (who gave me a second look), and over to the information desk.

The bank manager was Ted Myers. I knew him because I had gone to school with his kids. I told the receptionist that I was there to see him, and she led me back to his office.

Ted was a balding, taller gentleman now in his early sixties. His oldest son, Eric, had played football with Dickie. I went to school with his daughter, Susan and youngest son, Michael.

Ted was extremely fit for a sixty-year-old. When I walked into the office, he came over and gave me a big hug. "Bobby, I am so sorry to hear about Harry. Both I and Sharon are shocked and saddened," he said, referring to his wife. "If there is anything we can do, please let us know."

"Thank you, Mr. Myers. I spoke to Tom Zigelhofer yesterday and-"

"Yes, yes, you have some paperwork to sign," he reached into his desk and pulled out a bunch of documents and pushed them toward me.

"Harry signed his two savings accounts and checking accounts over to you. He came by a few days ago and made you the primary on all the accounts. I thought it rather odd, but he insisted. So, all you need to do is to sign, and you will be the primary account holder. We can transfer everything in your name, and if you like, keep the accounts active, which I hope you will consider."

I took the paperwork and read through it. In the primary savings account, Harry had socked away nearly $15,000 dollars. In the secondary savings – it looked to be a Christmas club – there was a little over $2,000 dollars. I signed both of the documents and handed them over to Ted.

He quickly scanned them. "Okay, this is fine. Will you want the accounts to remain open or will you like us to prepare a cashier's check?" he asked.

"Actually, I want it all in cash," I said.

It looked as though Ted Myers was about to have a heart attack.

"No, no," I laughed. "I was just kidding, Mr. Myers, let's leave the money here."

"Whew," he started. "I thought you were serious. I'll have one of the ladies prepare your savings books. They will be ready in just a moment. Now here is the paperwork for the checking account."

I looked them over and saw that Harry had left $1,800 dollars in the account. I had come into the bank with just a few dollars in my pocket, and I would leave with nearly twenty grand. For the time being, I definitely had to keep my financial windfall quiet. I signed the document and handed it back to him.

"This is all confidential, I assume?" I asked.

"Yes. Indeed. Now, do you need any cash?"

"Yes, I do. I need two-hundred dollars from the checking. I have some bills to take care of."

"Yes, I will get that right away. Here, just sign at the bottom of the withdrawal slip. Will twenties be okay?"

"That will be perfect. Is that all the business we have?" I asked.

"Oh, no. There are a few more matters. Harry set up a separate account for his funeral expenses. When he was diagnosed with cancer, he felt his time was short and set up the account a few months back. Your lawyer, Tom Zigelhofer will be administering that. Once all the expenses are paid, and any other outstanding debits taken from it, the remaining amount will be forwarded to you. Again, you can have it deposited in one of your existing accounts, or you can have a cashier's check drawn. It's your choice, but you don't have to decide right now. Okay, there are only two more things to discuss. Can we get you something to drink?" he offered.

"No, I'm good, Mr. Myers," I said. I liked this upper-crust treatment. I had never been treated with such respect in a bank before.

"Now, there is the matter of the house. Harry obtained his mortgage through us. We are also a title company. Next week, you can come in and have all the necessary paperwork done for both homes."

"Can anyone take them from me before the title is officially transferred?"

"No, if there are no liens against the properties – taxes, construction, those type of liens – and if the will has been properly filed with the courts, which it has, then no one can legally take the properties from you."

It was the 'legally' piece that worried me. In my neighborhood, legalities didn't matter so much.

"And one last thing. Here is the document you'll need to sign to access the safe-deposit box."

That caught me by surprise. I didn't know that Harry had a safe-deposit box. "Okay. Do you have the key?"

"Well, we have one key, but Harry told me the other day he had put your key away for safekeeping, and you would know where to find it. If you need a replacement key, well, that can be a problem. But we can get it replaced. It's just a pain in the butt. Why don't you try to find the key first before we go to the expense of replacing it?"

"Sure thing, Mr. Myers. I really appreciate everything that you've done." I got up and walked toward the door. Ted Myers followed me out of the bank. At the front door, he took my hand and shook it.

"Bobby, welcome to the bank. From here on out, you need to make sure you always make good decisions with your money. I don't think that will be a problem for you."

"Why do you think that, Mr. Myers?" I asked, a bit puzzled by his confidence in me.

"Because Harry told me the other day that you always make the right choices. Take care," he smiled, patted me on the back and returned to his office.

The way everything was unfolding was a bit strange. It seemed to me that Harry had already planned his death a few days before pulling the trigger. This was too much of a coincidence. He had changed his will just a few days before he killed himself. He also had gone through the trouble of getting all his financial affairs in order. So maybe it wasn't something or someone that prompted him. Maybe he had already determined the day and time that he would pull the trigger.

There was more to this story, and I felt that it would come out in the days ahead. At least, I hoped it would. I got into the car and pulled away from the bank to search for Jimmy.

***

I parked in Vivian's family's driveway. I couldn't park on the street in front of her house, because it was technically located on a state highway, and no parking was allowed. Fortunately, her father wasn't home – or at least the truck he drove wasn't in the driveway, so I took his spot, next to Vivian's mother's Olds Ninety-Eight.

I jumped out of the car and knocked on the front door. Vivian's mother, Mrs. Ann Mathis answered it. "Bobby," she sang, and pulled the door open. "I haven't seen you in such a long time. How are you doing?"

"I'm fine, Mrs. Mathis," I greeted, and entered the house. Vivian lived in an older home that was built around the turn of the century – similar to the house that I grew up in. They were odd-looking constructions, usually covered by shingle on the outside and consisting of two stories with a basement. However, they were very narrow. So, when I entered Vivian's home, all the rooms on the first floor, were to my left and directly to my right were the stairs leading to the second floor. I always felt a bit claustrophobic in these older turn of the century homes.

"I'm so glad to see you. To what do we owe the pleasure of this early-morning visit?" she asked.

"Well I stopped by to see if Vivian is here, Mrs. Mathis."

"Yes, she's upstairs. I heard her rustling about a few minutes ago. She's decent. Just go up. You still remember where her room is, don't you?"

I liked Mrs. Mathis. She was a realist. When I dated her daughter, she would often aid and abet me during our courtship. Old man Mathis was a hard ass and had protected his two daughters with an iron fist. So, whenever he caught me at the house, he would run me away. But soon afterwards, Mrs. Mathis would drop Vivian off at my house. She was a cool lady.

"Yes, I do remember, Mrs. Mathis," I said, and headed up the stairs.

"Well, I hope you kids can get back together..." she whispered, as I ran to the second floor. I didn't turn over her comment.

Vivian's room faced the street, which was good, because oftentimes I had to make my way out the house via the roof when Mr. Mathis would come home early from the mill.

When I got to the top of the stairs, I walked down the hall to the last room. I knocked on the door.

"Come in," Vivian said. I walked in the door. She was sitting on the edge of the bed in her panties and had a halter top barely dangling around her neck, loosely covering her breasts.

"Come on Vivian, let's not do this..." I protested, entering the room.

"Oh, I'm not doing anything. I bought this halter yesterday, and I wanted to see what it looked like. Could you tie it around my neck for me?"

"Sure," I walked over to her and tied the halter. She stood and looked in the mirror. "I don't like it," she proclaimed, quickly untied the halter and pulled it off. Her breasts fell out in front of me.

"Hand me my t-shirt on the bed," she requested, walking towards me topless. "Hey, you like my panties?" she asked. "They have a zipper, see," she said, and pulled the zipper down and quickly pulled it up.

I was doing all within my power to restrain myself. If Jimmy caught me, I was a dead man. This situation would be too hard to explain. "Hey, be good. Jimmy is my boy. I wouldn't do anything stupid to jeopardize our friendship."

"Not even if I got fully naked right now?"

"No, I'm not going to touch you. I have too much respect for Jimmy to touch his lady."

"And what if you saw me with another guy?"

"I would tell Jimmy, no question about it. So, put some clothes on and get decent."

"So why are you here?" she asked, pulling the t-shirt over her head. I was at least happy, though, that I got one last look at her breasts before she covered them.

"I need to find Jimmy."

"Okay. Jimmy," she said aloud, "Bobby needs to see you."

Jimmy quickly scooted from underneath the bed. I nearly shit in my pants when I saw him. He was grinning though, from ear to ear.

"My man, Bobby," he said, coming to his feet. He was wearing only his underwear.

"Why are you under the bed, Jimmy?"

"When I heard the door open downstairs, I thought you were Vivian's old man. But then I heard your voice, so I decided to stay under the bed to test you. And man, you passed the test."

"How wonderful for me," Vivian snapped, and pulled a pair of jeans over her panties.

"Why are you looking for me?"

"I suppose you heard about Harry?"

"The old dude that pulled the gun on me? No, what happened?"

"He killed himself on Wednesday."

"Wow, are you kidding me, Bobby? The old dude shot himself? Where?"

"In the head, right in his own bedroom."

Jimmy slapped me on the arm. "I'm sorry to hear that. That's some messed up shit. Are you all right?"

"I'm dealing with it," I said and looked over at Vivian. She was crying. She was always a very emotional person, and she genuinely liked Harry.

"When is the funeral?" she asked.

"Monday. The wake is at noon, and he'll be interred at 1:00 at Sunnyside."

"Nice place, Bobby. My mom is buried there," Jimmy said. "Now, why do you need me?"

"You remember on Tuesday evening when you came by to get Vivian?"

"Yeah. The old guy pulled a gun on me. How could I forget?" he laughed.

"Do you remember what type of gun he pulled on you?"

"Yeah, it was a small automatic. Like a .25 caliber. Nothing serious. That's why I was acting so courageous. I mean, if he had pulled a .357 or something like that on me, I would have pissed on myself."

I laughed. "Well, Doug claims that it was a Baretta."

"What the fuck does Doug know about guns? Hell, all he does is stay inside and watch TV. Maybe he saw a Baretta on Kojak," Jimmy laughed.

"He's giving me some grief right now, so do you mind stopping by the house tomorrow to straighten this out?" I asked.

"Just tell me what time, and I will be there."

"I'll call you. Hey, I appreciate this, man," I said and shook his hand.

"Don't worry about it. You're my boy, so it's not a problem. Just call me and I'll come around."

"You know that Doug is going to be pissed though," I warned Jimmy.

"I'm not worried about Doug. You know I can kick his ass in my sleep."

"Yes, I suspect you can. Look, I have to run. There are some folk at the house that are waiting on me to return. Can I give you anything?"

Jimmy laughed. "I can't take any money from you. Well, not today I can't. Not after what I heard in this room. You're a standup guy. We'll always be cool – that is as long as you don't try to sleep with my lady," he laughed.

"Later, Jimmy," I said and shook his hand. I walked over to Vivian and gave her a kiss on the cheek. "I'll see you on Monday, Viv."

Vivian smiled. "I'll be there, Bobby."

As I was walking out the room, Jimmy stopped me. "Hey, Bobby."

I turned. "Yeah, Jimmy?"

"Keep your ears open. I hear your brother Dickie might be involved in some mob type of shit. So make sure you and the rest of your family are looking over your shoulders. You never know about those goombahs."

"Mob, huh?"

"Yeah, Cleveland mob. At least, that is what I heard. So keep an eye out, okay?"

"Thanks for the heads-up, Jimmy."

I said good-bye and left the house.

***

When I pulled back into the driveway, I saw Eleanor sitting on the front porch. She didn't look happy. I sensed trouble. I opened the car door and as soon as my foot touched the gravel I could hear screaming and yelling from the kitchen. One of the voices I recognized as Dickie's. The other, was unfamiliar to me, so I assumed it was Eleanor's husband, son, or brother.

I walked over to the house. "What's going on here?" I asked, the screaming from the kitchen nearly drowning me out.

"You know what's going on. How did you do it? How did you get him to sign it all over to you?"

"Oh, that again. Look, lady, I don't know you, and I'm not comfortable discussing my personal business with you..." Just then I heard a loud crash and a man scream in pain. I ignored Eleanor and ran into the house.

In the middle of the living room floor, Dickie was on top of Eleanor's son and wailing him. Doug was holding both older men back. Denise was quietly sitting on the couch watching the commotion.

"Dickie, stop this," I yelled, and grabbed him.

Dickie was pissed. "Fuck that, Bobby. This asshole deserves to have his ass kicked. He called you a fucking thief. I'm not going to stand by and let anyone call any member of my family a thief. You understand, punk?" Dickie screamed and punched Phillip in the mouth.

"Dickie, leave him alone," I pulled him off of Phillip. Phillip jumped up from the floor, bleeding from the mouth and plopped on the couch. He used his shirt to blot the blood that was trickling from the corner of his mouth.

"That wasn't called for," he protested, trying to stop the bleeding. His sister, Chandra, was in the kitchen, sitting at the table and quietly drinking a cup of coffee.

Eleanor walked inside the house, behind me and screamed, "He called you a thief because that's what you are."

"Mama, stay out of it," Phillip implored. "There's been enough of this."

"Ma'am", I started, "You don't know me. I found out yesterday that Harry had left these things to me. It all came as a shock. I'm willing to discuss everything rationally, but I'm not going to do this now. On Monday, after the funeral, I'll sit down with everyone, and we can work this out. But now, we need to continue to prepare for a funeral. Harry's dead, people. Doesn't that mean anything to you all?" I finished and walked out the room and went directly to the basement.

Harry had been building a bar in the basement. It was a project that he never completed. But he stocked it with a few brands of drink. I grabbed a bottle of whiskey off the shelf and poured myself a shot.

"Pour me one, as well," a female voice said from behind me. It was Chandra. She had followed me downstairs. "I could use a drink."

I pulled another shot glass off the shelf and poured. We touched glasses.

"I can never get used to this stuff," I said, sitting my empty glass on the bar. I walked over to the couch that Harry had put in the basement. I took a seat on it and continued, "This was supposed to be Harry's man cave. He never completed it. When I came home on the weekends to visit my mother, I would help him with the project."

"I didn't know my uncle Harry very well. Apparently, you two were very close," Chandra said.

"We were okay. I respected Harry, and he respected me. We never had words. I always treated him with the upmost respect. He deserved no less."

"I see," Chandra said, sitting next to me on the couch.

"I always treated him like a man. All men, regardless of their age, want to be treated with worth and dignity. That's all Harry wanted. When he got the cancer, he began to slow down, but he never wanted that to be an excuse. I made sure I continued to push him."

"You cared for him a lot, didn't you?"

"Of course. He was a good man, and I'll miss him every day for the rest of my life."

She smiled and said, "You're very kind and seem to be a bit calmer than your brother, Dickie. He's quite the hothead."

I laughed. "True, but I can say the same about Phillip. Taking on Dickie is a courageous, but foolish thing to do. Dickie has never lost a fight in his life – at least not one that I'm aware of."

"Well, then his streak continues because based on what I could see, he kicked the shit out of Phil."

I laughed. "Well, I'm sorry that happened, but my family is very close-knit and we don't take insults well," I said, and decided to lay all my cards on the table. "Look, regardless of what you might think, I am not a crook or thief. I didn't know anything about this until after Harry died. I had no idea he would leave everything to me."

"Well he did, and now that it is done, what are you going to do with it all?"

I didn't know where she was going with this. "I'm going to do exactly what Harry would want me to do."

"And what's that?"

"I'm going to make good decisions," I answered.

She turned and kissed me on the cheek. "I'm sure you will," she said, and left.

"Strange," I whispered softly, as she disappeared up the stairs. I took another shot of whiskey and drifted into deep thoughts.

***

When I finally returned to the upstairs, things had quieted down quite a bit. In fact, Doug, Phillip, Denise and Chandra were huddled around the kitchen table playing a game of backgammon. Herbert and Paul had nodded off, on the couch. I went into the living room and looked out the front door. Eleanor was sitting on the porch. I assumed Dickie was either taking a nap or was in the bathroom.

I opened the screen door and stepped outside, onto the porch. Eleanor looked up at me. She was sitting in my mother's favorite chair. I called it "Mom's Nosey Chair," because on a warm day, my mother would sit in this chair for hours and watch who was coming and going in the neighborhood. I took a seat in the chair next to Eleanor.

"I'm sorry about earlier," she apologized. "I hope there are no hard feelings."

"Don't worry about it. I'm good. I have been called far worse than that," I laughed.

"Chandra had a talk with me. She says that you have a kind heart."

"Yeah, here lately I keep hearing how kind I am. It makes me a bit paranoid."

"There's nothing wrong with being a good person, son."

"Well, your brother was a good person. In fact, he was one of the best men I've ever met. You might not believe it, but I loved him, and he was more of a father to me that my biological dad."

81

"What happened to your father?" she asked.

"He's around. He lives out of the state. He and Ma didn't work out. So they divorced. I haven't heard from him in years," I explained.

"Well, he's missing out," she said.

"How's that?"

"You've turned out to be quite the young man. He is missing out on that. My daughter tells me that you cared quite a bit about Harry."

Eleanor and Chandra apparently had adopted a 'be nice to Bobby' strategy. I guessed they felt that by doing so, it would be easier for them to ask me for the house. I really didn't care about much of anything at this point, except honoring the legacy of Harry Bremen. And the best way I could do that was to make good choices about his estate and what lie ahead for me in my future.

"I did. Not only was Harry like a father to me, he was also my friend," I said, and then decided I had said enough. "I need to get some rest, but when my mom returns home, we can sit down and talk about everything," I offered.

"That'll be fine with me. What time do you expect your mother to return from her trip?" She asked.

"The graduation ceremony should be over by now. She mentioned staying until Saturday morning, but I think they'll probably come home tonight. I figure she'll be on the highway in the next hour or so. I think she should be here by four or five."

"Well, I look forward to seeing Sarah again. We haven't spoken since the family reunion last summer."

And I knew how well that had gone, I said to myself. My mother wasn't going to be happy that Eleanor and her clan were staying with us. I could imagine the things she would say and accuse them of when she returned. It wasn't going to be pretty. "I'm sure my mom is looking forward to seeing you," I lied.

I sat there for a few awkward minutes, not quite sure what to say. Eleanor didn't seem to latch onto my last comment, so I figured she must have thought that it was disingenuous.

"Well, I think I will go inside and see if I can get some rest. That is if I can get Dickie out of the guest room," I smiled and started to stand.

"Your brother, Dickie?" she questioned.

"Yes, Dickie."

"He left about ten minutes ago, before you came up from the basement."

I stood up and peered over the hedges that shrouded the front porch from the street. The Malibu was still there.

"Did he walk somewhere?" I asked her.

"No, he had a ride. I was sitting here, and this nice car pulled up. He walked out to it and said something to the driver. Then he looked toward the house for a second and jumped in the back seat."

That wasn't good news, and it worried me. "Did you see who was driving the car or if anyone else was in it?" I panicked a bit. Jimmy's advice was fresh in my mind.

"No, the windows were tinted so I couldn't see inside."

Shit, I thought to myself. "Excuse me," I said and walked past Eleanor and went into the house. Doug was still at the kitchen table playing backgammon.

"Doug," I whispered. He looked up from the table, and I waved him into the living room.

"What's up, Bobby?" he asked, irritated that I lured him from his game.

"Did you see who Dickie left with?"

"Dickie's not here?"

"Fuck," I snapped. "Damn, Doug, couldn't you keep an eye on him. Mrs. Thurman said that he got into a nice car about ten minutes ago. Shit, this can't be good."

"I wouldn't worry. You know Dickie. He is always going somewhere."

"God damn, Doug are you that fucking obtuse? Geez, I can't believe you man. Didn't Dickie tell you what was going on when you, he and Denise came up with the scheme to shake me down for money?"

"He mentioned he owed some money and could use the cash. He didn't give any details."

"Doug, hello..." I said, a bit sarcastically, "Dickie wasn't late on something like a car loan. He owes some bad people money, and they want him to pay up. He's been trying to keep low and out of sight for a few days. Shit, this isn't good. He could be in danger."

"Oh hell, Bobby. You're worrying for nothing. You know Dickie has all kinds of friends here. He could be out with anyone."

"And tell me, Einstein," I yelled, "What fucking friend would Dickie have here in town that wouldn't come into the house to offer their condolences? Who does he know in this town that we don't know? God Damn, you're fucking useless sometimes. You need to plug in with the real world."

"And you need to ease up and pull back on me a little. I'm your brother, not your bitch," Doug snapped.

"Sometimes I wonder," I cursed, and walked away. Doug ran up behind me and grabbed me by the shoulder and jerked me around forcefully. I turned and brought my fist across his jaw, and he dropped to the floor, onto his knees.

In the meanwhile, an audience had assembled to watch the small ruckus. "Shit," Doug moaned, rubbing his chin. "I just wanted to ask you a question, that's all."

"We need to find Dickie. We need to find him right now," I screamed and walked past Doug and went into the kitchen. I had to locate Dickie before our mother came home. I picked up the phone and dialed.

"Hello," Vivian answered.

"Viv, it's Bobby. Let me speak to Jimmy."

"He's not here. He got some phone call and ran out of here like a bat flying out of hell, Bobby. He looked worried."

"And he didn't mention where he was going."

"No."

"Who knew that he was at your house?"

"I don't know who it was that called him...hold on," she said, and in the background I heard her yell to her mom and asked who had called Jimmy. Her mom said something that I couldn't make out. "My mom says that she didn't recognize the voice. But it was a guy. Is everything all right?"

"Yeah, everything is cool. Look, if you see Jimmy or hear from him, tell him that I'm looking for him, okay?"

"Sure thing, Bobby. But I sense a little worry in your voice. Seriously, are you okay?"

"I'm fine, Vivian. Look, I'll call you later and explain. I have to run. Take care."

I hung up the phone. Doug was standing behind me with a worried look on his face. I glanced at the clock on the wall. It was just a little past 1:00 in the afternoon.

"Nothing?" Doug asked.

"No. Vivian said that Jimmy ran out of her house in a hurry. She doesn't know where he is at. We need to find Dickie."

"Where do you plan on looking?"

"Come outside with me," I requested. Doug followed me as we walked to the front lawn, out of earshot of the folk in the house. "Look, I'm sorry about what I said to you inside the house," I apologized. "I'm worried about Dickie. Jimmy told me that Dickie owed the mob some money and to keep an eye out for anything unusual."

"Okay, so where do we start?"

"You stay here in case he comes back. I'm going down to see old man Carlucci to see if he has heard anything," I said.

"Armand Carlucci, huh? I haven't talked to him in a few years," Doug said.

"Usually when I'm home I go by and see him," I said.

Armand Carlucci was a local Italian-American businessman who owned two beer and wine carryouts in our small town. I had known Armand since I was a little kid – having been his paperboy for a number of years. I liked him so much that I would make his store the last stop on my paper route and would sit with him and have a cold soda and listen to his stories about growing up in Italy.

We had a good history. When I turned sixteen, I worked the carryout for him when he had to run errands. And for some reason, even though I was under age, I never had a problem selling beer and wine to the locals. I knew he had mob connections – in fact, sometimes I believed that he was a part of the organization. Often, when I was in the store with him, many questionable characters would show up, and he would ask me to leave for the day while he discussed business.

Armand was always packed heat. I don't know what type of gun he carried, but he was always ready for any type of trouble. During the Teamsters truckers' strike back in the early seventies, while no one was able to get any goods into their stores, Armand was fully stocked with beer, wine, snacks, and the hard stuff.

"Keep the Thurmans entertained, if you can. And tell Denise where I'm going," I said to Doug.

"I'll do that. Call me though, if you need me."

I jumped into the Malibu, pulled out of the driveway and then gunned the engine.

***

I drove to the northwest side of town. Armand usually worked in his carryout nearest my old neighborhood. His daughter worked his other place, on the west side of town.

The carryout, which was actually a drive-through, was a short ten minute drive away. I drove to the rear where cars entered the store and saw Armand's car. I parked next to it, turned off my car and ran into the store.

Armand was sitting in a chair next to the cash register. There were no customers inside. He looked up as I walked towards him.

Armand was a short, olive skinned man, and despite being in the country for over thirty-five years, still spoke with a thick accent. He stood up and walked over to me.

"Bobby," he said, as I neared, and extended his hand.

I shook it. "Armand, I need your help. Have you seen Dickie?"

Armand smiled. "Sit down, Bobby, and we'll discuss your brother."

Shit, I thought. Just as I figured. Armand knew something. "Armand, I'm too nervous to sit. Just tell me what's going on?"

"Sit down, Bobby, and we'll talk," he said a little more forcefully. I was

86

worried, but I wasn't going to disrespect him. I sat in a folding chair.

Armand picked his chair up and positioned it across from me. He reached up and hit the door control, and the rear door came down. "I don't want any interruptions during our chat," he smiled.

I was in a near panic. My heart was pounding, but I couldn't come across as impatient with Armand. I needed to hear him out. "So, what's going on, Armand?" I tried again.

"Yes, I have seen your brother. He was here a few minutes ago with a few associates of mine."

"Is he okay?" I asked.

"Yes. But that stupid brother of yours is in a fix. He owes some business associates of mine a lot of money. And, Bobby, he has to pay."

"How much does he owe?" I asked. I was careful not to implicate Armand in this. Clearly, he was somehow involved, but only as a middle man or go between. Maybe Dickie had used Armand as a reference or something. I wasn't sure.

"A lot of money. It seems your brother likes to gamble. So, he is in to these gentlemen for some serious cash."

"I have money, Armand. I can help," I offered. I loved my brother Dickie, and even though he could be an asshole, I couldn't stand by and let something happen to him.

"Bobby, I heard your stepfather died a few days ago," he started. I couldn't believe he was ignoring me.

"Yes, he did," I answered as patiently as I could.

"Well my condolences to you, your mother and your family. This is tragic news."

"Thank you, Armand. I appreciate your kind sentiments."

"So you have money to pay this debt that your brother has made?"

"It depends on the amount, but I have the money."

"And you would pay your brother's debt?" he asked.

"Yes sir, I wouldn't hesitate to do it."

Armand thought for a moment. Then he looked at me and said, "You have been around me long enough to know that this is not about the money. It is about a man's word. Your brother placed bets with these gentlemen, and they took him on his word that he would make good on his losses. Then he tried to skip out on his debts. Bobby, this is no way to do business. A man honors his debts. Always understand that."

"I do, but you know Dickie. So, I'll help pay, okay?"

"Bobby, this is Dickie's debt to pay. I won't take your money personally, but I will discuss it with these associates of mine."

"Armand, please, this is my brother. I can't sit by and let any harm come to him."

Armand laughed. "Bobby, because we are Italians you think we are going to harm him?"

You're go• •amn right, I thought to myself. "I'm sorry, Armand. Really, I am. But please-"

"Sometimes Bobby, things are not as obvious as one might think. Dickie's fate is not in my hands. It is in his hands. I will tell my associates about your offer. What you can do for Dickie is to go home now," Armand suggested.

"Armand, why can't we get this resolved today?" I asked. I was a bit desperate because though Armand had said that no harm would come to Dickie; I wasn't quite sure I believed him.

"Bobby," Armand said, getting up from his chair and grabbing my arm. "I know that he is your brother. And you have come to me in good faith to plead on his behalf. And as I have told you, I will take your offer and present it to my associates. But remember, this is Dickie's debt to pay, and I'm sure that he and my associates can work out an amicable agreement without your involvement."

"Armand, don't let them hurt my brother."

"If he pays his debt, from what I know about these people, then they won't hurt him. But go home now. If I hear anything else about your brother, I will call you."

"Armand, are you sure that you can't take the money and offer it up? Really, there's nothing else that you can do?"

"Go home, Bobby. Remember, things are not always as they seem," he said, and then pressed the opener, and the rear overhead door lifted.

This cloak-and-dagger bullshit coming from Armand unnerved me. I wanted to press if further, but aggravating Armand wasn't something I should do at this point. If he said he would speak to his associates on my behalf, I believed him. But this thing about things not always appearing to be the case bothered me. What did he mean by that?

But, I let it go and left the drive-through. I stopped short of the exit and turned back around to Armand, but he waved me on. I sensed that Armand wasn't giving me the entire story. I couldn't believe that he would turn down the money. So I left somewhat confused. I didn't know what I was going to tell my mother.

***

When I returned home, the green Chrysler was in the driveway, so our mother and Stephanie had returned. It was nearly six o'clock in the evening. I wasn't sure how I would handle the Dickie situation with my mother.

I got out of the car and walked toward the house. The kitchen window was opened, and I could hear pleasantries drifting out of it into the evening air. I recognized my mother's and Eleanor's voices chatting as though they were the oldest and dearest of friends.

I went into the house. Phillip, Herbert and Paul were sitting on the couch. Doug darted towards me from one of the back rooms.

"Did you get any information on Dickie?" he asked.

I nodded to Doug. I didn't want to discuss my meeting with Armand in the open, so we slipped past the kitchen, and went into the guest bedroom. Doug closed the door behind us.

"So, what did you learn?" he asked.

"Armand would tell me only that Dickie owes some people some money, and he has to pay," I explained.

"And did you offer to pay this money, after all-"

"These guys don't work that way, or at least not Armand. He told me that he wouldn't take my money. This is Dickie's debt. But he did say that he would take my offer to his associates."

Doug looked at me for a minute and then I saw him make a fist. Before I could take a breath, it was rushing to my face. I grabbed it just before it landed on my chin.

"What the fuck is wrong with you?" I asked angrily, and threw his arm to the side.

"You cheap fucker. You are letting this money go to your head. How can you tell a fucking lie like that? Do you think I'm stupid?"

"If you think I'm lying you can go and talk to Armand. He'll tell you the same thing that he told me. So, look, call me what you want, but I would never allow harm to come to any of my brothers or sisters when I can do something to prevent it. Calm down, okay?"

"Okay," Doug muttered, disarmed, and sat down on the bed.

"Look, while Armand takes this proposal to his boys, maybe we can work out our own deal. I'm thinking if we can locate where these guys are, maybe we can just give the money directly to them."

"And how are we going to find out who and where they are?"

"I don't know. I need to think about it. I still have a call out to Jimmy, so maybe he can point us in the right direction. After all, he was the one who gave me the tip in the first place."

"Okay, we start there. In the meantime, what do we tell Mama?" he asked.

"We just tell her that Dickie left with some friends. Eleanor was out front when he left and can back us up on that. Even so, all this depends on how you handled it with the rest of the family when we had our little fight earlier."

"I told them that Dickie got into the car with some old friends, and that you were blowing this all out of proportion. They seemed to buy it."

"And how has Mom been acting since she returned?"

"She's actually been pretty decent with her guests. As far as I can tell she's treated everyone kindly. Something tells me, though, this is the calm before the storm," Doug said.

I laughed. I had started to feel a little better. And of course, I had no choice but to feel better because I had to put a strong face on for my mother. If I didn't, she would see right through me and know that something was wrong. "Well, knowing Mom, the other shoe is going to drop soon. And when it does..."

"Boom," Doug said.

"Okay, let me go talk to her. It's strange she hasn't asked about Dickie yet."

"She will. So we might as well go face the music," Doug suggested.

We left the room and entered the kitchen just as my mother got up from the table to put her coffee cup into the sink. My mother was a coffee addict. She drank five or six cups daily. When I stepped into the kitchen, she stopped and turned to greet me. "Hey, honey. Where have you been?"

"I was just running some errands," I lied and glanced over at Eleanor. I wanted to see her reaction. She didn't seem to turn it over at all. I turned back to my mother.

"Have you seen Dickie?" my mom continued.

"No, Ma'am. He left a little while ago with some friends. I'm sure he won't be gone long because he knew you might come back tonight. How was the graduation?"

"It was good. Your sister was beautiful in her cap and gown," my mother answered.

Just then, Laura came up from downstairs and ran towards me. She gave me a big hug. I was really happy to see her and even happier that she chose that moment to interrupt my conversation with our mother.

"I missed you today, big brother," she smiled. "It wasn't the same without you."

"Mom wanted me to stay behind to help take care of the home front," I smiled and gave her a kiss on the forehead.

"So how is Bobby?" she asked, taking my hand and leading me out to the front porch, away from it all. She knew me well, and I am sure she could see in my face that I wanted to be anywhere but in the kitchen. I was relieved that she rescued me from further interrogation.

The evening air had chilled. We sat on the porch.

"I'm fine, Sis, and I'm so sorry I couldn't be there for you today," I answered. Laura was absolutely my favorite sister.

"What you had to do here was more important, Bobby. And hey, I heard that Harry signed everything over to you, and I think that's wonderful. Of course, Mom, Stephanie and all those strange people in the house right now don't share the same sentiment. I think it's neat."

"Oh, that reminds me," I said, and reached in my back pocket and pulled out the two hundred dollars in cash that I had earlier, withdrawn from the bank.

"Here, happy graduation. I know it's not much, but it's a start until I get all this legal stuff worked out."

"Bobby, this is very generous. Thank you so much," she said and gave me a kiss on the cheek.

"Look, there's more to come as..."

"This is more than enough," she interrupted.

"Okay, but if you need more, let me know."

"I don't need any more," she smiled and gave me a hug.

"So, I see Mom is getting along with our visitors. What gives?" I asked, amused.

Laura laughed along with me and said, "Yes, I'm as surprised as you are that she's getting along with these folks. I thought for sure when we pulled up, and they introduced themselves that all hell was going to break loose. But so far, she has been rather..."

Our conversation was abruptly interrupted by a car pulling onto our front lawn. I jumped up from the porch just as the front of the car skipped the curb and lunged forward onto the grass. It unexpectedly skidded across the lawn coming to a stop just inches short of the green Chrysler. Vivian was driving, and she seemed to be in a panic.

I ran across the lawn to the driver's side and opened the door. "Vivian, are you okay," I yelled, grabbing her by the arm to help her out the car. Then I noticed that she was sobbing and asked, "Vivian, what's wrong?"

She looked up at me. Her face was nearly black from her eyeliner. "It's Jimmy," she sobbed and almost fell out of the car onto the grass.

"Viv, what about Jimmy?" I asked.

She looked up at me and with sad, sullen eyes, said, "I can't find him, and I've looked everywhere and called everyone. I think something bad may have happened to him."

***

We managed to calm Vivian, help her out the car, and get her into the kitchen. My mother made her a cup of tea and then shooed everyone out of the kitchen, except Laura and me. I was surprised that Vivian was so upset. For one, Jimmy always went missing. He was involved in so many illegal activities that he often fell off the grid. And secondly, I really didn't think she was as committed to Jimmy as she now appeared to be.

Mom sat a cup of tea in front of her. "Vivian, drink this tea. It'll make you feel better."

She looked up and said, "Thank you, Mrs. Bremen."

"So, what's going on, Vivian?" I asked, as she took a sip from the cup.

"I'm worried about Jimmy," she said.

My mom sat down at the table. "Honey, does he disappear from time to time?"

"Yes he does, but he always tells me where he's going and when he'll return. So I don't worry. Since we've been dating, Mrs. Bremen, he has never gone a full day without telling me where he might be. I've called everyone I know and searched everywhere, and I can't find him."

"But why do you think something bad might have happened to him?" I asked.

"Bobby, I went by his place, and it was torn up. Someone had been in there searching for something. I called the police and Jackson came, and they searched the place. And..." she choked, and took a drink of tea. She cried.

"Hey, it's okay," Laura chimed in. "Come on, tell us about it. Maybe we can help."

"They found blood on the kitchen floor, and the back door was left open. Jackson says it looks as though someone was dragged down the stairs."

"Do you think he went to his place after he got the telephone call? You, know, the call you told me about?" I asked.

"I'm not sure. Usually when he is in trouble, he goes home and packs a bag. I looked into his bedroom closet, and his suitcase is missing. So I'm not sure what happened. Jackson thinks someone might have come up on him when he was packing. It's so terrible. What am I going to do?" she sobbed.

For some reason, when I heard her story, I got a bad feeling inside. I somehow felt that Jimmy's disappearance and Dickie's ride were related.

"Vivian, there's nothing we can do tonight," my mom said. "You should go home and rest."

"I don't want to go home. My mom and dad went away for the weekend, and I feel a little weird about staying alone."

"You can stay here, sweetheart," my mom said. "We have plenty of room."

I didn't know what she meant by plenty, because as it stood right now, we were about two deep in every room. But this was Vivian, and she was my friend. So we would make room.

"Thank you, Mrs. Bremen. I know this is a lot to ask, especially during this difficult time for you. I appreciate it so much," Vivian said.

"Don't think anything else about it. You are always welcome in my home, Vivian," my mother said, getting up from the table.

Mom looked over at me. "Do you think we will hear from your brother before the night is over?" she asked. There was a hint of suspicion in her voice.

"I guess he plans on spending the night with his friends. I haven't heard from him."

"Let's hope we hear from him soon," she glared at me and left the room.

I turned to Vivian. "Hey, I'll set you up with some space in the basement. Most of us are sleeping down there. We're all slumming it, so we can make do."

She gave me a kiss. "Thank you, Bobby. Do you think tomorrow you can help me find Jimmy?"

"Sure, after we get through the personal family stuff, I'll drive you around town. I'm certain he's going to turn up tomorrow."

"I hope so."

I grabbed some blankets from the linen closet and led her downstairs. Everyone was lounging around and looked a little irritated when I made room on the floor for Vivian. But no one said anything. They were all involved in their own personal conversations and seemingly ignoring the others. Chandra was in a corner talking to her brother Phillip. Laura, Denise and Doug were sprawled out on the couch deep in conversation. And Stephanie was on the floor playing a card game with Tanya.

"I hope I'm not imposing," Vivian said when she saw the crowd.

"It's not a problem," I said and put a few blankets on the floor. "Are you okay?"

"I am now," she said with a smile and gave me a hug. "Thank you," she whispered in my ear.

I genuinely liked Vivian and as much as she needed me, I needed her as well. I relied on her friendship.

"I'm glad, Vivian. We need to get some sleep," I suggested and then chased my sisters and Doug off the couch. I had marked out my territory earlier. I flopped onto the couch, grabbed a blanket, and while the others continued to talk, I drifted off.

DAY 5 – SATURDAY

During the early hours of Saturday morning I had an amazing dream. I dreamt that someone came to me during the night, unzipped my pants, pulled down my shorts, and orally caressed my privates. But when I woke up at nine in the morning, I felt strangely damp in my groin area. When I reached down under my covers to check it out, I embarrassingly found my pants unzipped. So, I began to doubt if my dream had really been a dream or actual fellatio. I looked around the room and fortunately, everyone was still asleep, so I zipped my pants, and hurriedly jumped off the couch.

I went up the stairs to the kitchen. My mother, Eleanor, Herbert, and Paul were sitting at the table, having a cup of coffee. Besides me, they were the only ones stirring in the house.

I was actually quite proud of my mother. I had expected her to be a bit bitchy and hard to get along with. But surprisingly, she had been, thus far, quite pleasant. It was my hope that she would be able to maintain this posture throughout the Thurman's visit, but I wasn't optimistic. A storm was brewing inside of her. It was only a matter of time.

"Good morning," I greeted, as I walked through the kitchen.

"Good morning, Bobby," a chorus of greetings filled the room.

"Bobby, have a seat and join us for a cup of coffee," my mother offered.

Oh great, the forces had aligned during my sleep, and now I was going to be grilled from divergent sides of the family – folk, who during normal circumstances would rather spit on each other than speak - had now, during financial windfall days formed allegiances for the good of their purses and wallets. Their motives were transparent, but having a cup of coffee with them might prove amusing.

"Okay," I agreed, and took a seat next to my mother and directly across from Eleanor. Paul was to my left, at the end of the table and Herbert sat next to Eleanor.

Paul nodded at me and smiled. When I looked at him, he shied away from my glance, picked up his cup of coffee and took a drink.

"Bobby, have you thought about what you are going to do with these properties that Harry left in your care?" my mother asked, breaking the awkwardness of the situation.

"Nope," I started, taking a sip of coffee. "I haven't really thought about it yet." And it was the truth. At that point, I had not given the properties much thought. Dickie and Jimmy were top of mind for me.

"Well, honey, don't you think this is something that you should give some thought to?" Eleanor asked. Her question shocked me, not because of the nature of the question, but because this was something that I felt was a personal matter. I had only met this woman twenty-four hours earlier. More surprisingly though, was how calm my mother remained while Eleanor floated the question to me. I concluded then that this intervention of sorts was contrived and poorly planned.

"I'll get around to it soon. But here's the deal. I believe that Harry left these things to me because he felt that whatever I did with them, I would be fair. And, I intend to be," I said.

"Bobby, we're not trying to upset you," my mother said calmly.

"Maybe you aren't, Mom, but this is neither the time nor place to discuss this. For one, and please, forgive me," I started and turned to Eleanor, "but I don't know you people. I hope that doesn't offend you, but quite frankly, I'm a bit uncomfortable discussing this with strangers. And secondly, I'm not ready to discuss it with anyone. While I understand that everyone is a bit anxious..."

"Well, with all due respect, young man, we are a bit anxious because this is our life. You must think it's a game," Herbert accused.

Eleanor glared at Herbert. He closed his mouth and turned away.

"And with all due respect to you, sir, my stepfather is down at Spencer's

Funeral Home. And if you didn't know, or if you needed reminding, he shot himself a few days ago. And while life might easily go on for you, well, at the moment, it is a bit disruptive for me. Because, you see," I yelled, standing and then shoving the chair under the table, "I loved that old guy."

"Bobby, please, calm down," my mother said.

"I don't understand why this is something that can't wait for a day or two," I started, pissed at the lot of them. And then the doorbell rang.

"What's with the fucking doorbell every morning," I screamed. "Every morning the goddamn doorbell rings," I yelled.

I was becoming unraveled. This thing with Harry – the actual suicide – and the weight of the inheritance was just too much for me to bear at the moment. Everyone was walking around me like a pack of wolves, ready to pounce for a piece of meat. My thoughts of Harry were working on me. I was mentally exhausted. And now, I had to deal with another fucking doorbell. "Shit," I screamed.

No one made a move for the door, because as I had come to realize, no one in the household was capable of answering the door, except me. However, in this instance, I guess I didn't blame them. They were all looking at me - drop jawed, with shocked and dismayed expressions on their faces. "I guess I'll get that," I snapped and went to the front door.

I jerked open the front door and looked through the screen. Standing on the porch were a short, pudgy brunette, with far too much make-up smeared on her face, accompanied by a slender, thin, blonde companion who looked as though he had not visited a dentist in quite a spell.

"Yeah, what can I do for you?" I asked.

"Is this the Bremen residence?" she asked.

"Yes, this is," I answered as my mother came up behind me to investigate.

"My name is Eileen. And Harry Bremen was my father."

***

After our new visitors' revelation, I had immediately called Ziegelhofer to see if he knew anything about Eileen. When I hung the phone up I returned to the living room where my mother, Eleanor, and the rest of the Bremen and Thurman elders were interrogating the visitor. Eileen's boyfriend, or companion, or whatever he was, stayed on the porch. I went over to my mother and whispered into her ear, "Tom said he has never heard of her. He said Harry never mentioned her."

"Eileen, you'll have to forgive us but Harry never told me that he had an illegitimate child," my mother said, getting in her subtle dig.

"I'm sorry to shock you all like this, but Harry Bremen was my father."

I decided to let my mother and the other elders, handle the new visitor and her declaration while I went and had a shower. This was just perfect – and something I should have expected. Of course, there would be a long-lost heir who stepped in from out of the shadows just two days before the funeral. It was perfect timing.

My mother continued her intense interrogation and was ably assisted by her sister-in-law. When I finished my shower and dressed, I walked back into the room, and they were still questioning the young lady. I was uninterested in what was going on, ignored their impromptu inquisition, and went to the basement. I was confident that if they needed me, they would call me.

Now that there was a new commotion, everyone was upstairs with my mother investigating. So, I had the basement, and my thoughts, to myself.

Harry spent a lot of time in the basement. While he was always very private about his life, he did share a few things with me during our moments together.

His intention had been to make the basement his place. He had devoted half of it to his work area and laundry room. That part he had left unfinished. The other half, he had started to finish and had managed to get most of the work done, having put in walnut paneled walls, ceiling tile, and carpeting. The basement opened out, via a sliding door, to the backyard.

He put a barbeque grill just outside the sliding door and had mentioned to me that he was going to run a natural-gas line into the backyard to hook up a permanent grill. But first, he had wanted to complete his bar.

The bar, built from plywood, was still very rough. Before Harry had been able to finish the bar, the cancer diagnosis had come, suddenly slowing him down. So, it just sat, unfinished, in the corner of the wonderful den that he had built. I thought maybe I could continue his work and finish the bar, but decided against it. In some way, I figured that the unfinished bar would always be a memorial to Harry.

I plopped on the couch and began to survey my thoughts when I heard someone coming down the stairs. I opened my eyes just as Vivian and Chandra came into the room and sat next to me on the couch – Chandra on my right, Vivian on my left.

I was a little embarrassed because I really didn't know what to say to either one of them after what had happened the previous night.

"It looks like your old girlfriend and I have a few things in common," Chandra said, and placed her hand on my thigh.

"I can imagine," I started. "So, what do I owe the pleasure of this visit by you two lovely ladies?"

"I just wanted to thank you for letting me stay the night," Vivian said.

"It wasn't me. It was my mother," I smiled.

"It was you," Vivian said, and nudged me.

"So, are you okay today?" I asked.

"I'm doing better. Later, will you still go out with me and look for Jimmy?"

"I haven't forgotten."

"Do you mind if I ride along with you two?" Chandra asked.

"Of course not. The more the merrier," I agreed. I didn't see a downside to hanging out with two beautiful women. My thoughts began to imagine all types of scenarios, but I was abruptly returned to reality by one simple question from Chandra.

"Are you gay?" she asked. The question hit me in the head like a hammer, and I almost fell to the floor.

Vivian laughed when she heard the question. "I didn't see that coming," she howled.

"Why would you ask that question?" I asked, puzzled. I wondered what on earth I could have done that gave her that impression.

"Then maybe you and Vivian are seeing each other?" she pressed.

Vivian smiled. "I have someone."

Chandra turned to me. "Don't get me wrong. I'm not trying to be conceited, but I think I'm fairly attractive and, Bobby, you haven't shown the slightest interest in me."

"Look, first of all, I'm not a homosexual. I like women. Tell her, Vivian."

Vivian laughed. "I never thought I would ever have to validate this. No, Bobby is not gay. Why would you think that?"

"I don't know, Bobby just hasn't shown any interest in me," Chandra said.

"That leads me to my second point. I think you are very attractive but right now my mind is on burying my stepfather and settling his affairs. So, don't take my lack of attention as disinterest. That's not the case, okay," I said.

"Thanks for explaining that. I'm not sure it makes me feel any better, but hey, a girl has to try sometimes, right, Vivian?"

Vivian laughed. "Certainly. We can't risk letting good men get away."

"Yes, there are so few of them," Chandra chimed in with laughter.

"Yeah, okay, girls. Give it a break..." I said.

But before I could continue with my thought, I heard footsteps. I looked up and saw that my brother Doug and three sisters were coming down the stairs.

"Excuse me ladies, but my sisters and I need to talk to our brother in private. I hope you don't mind. This won't take long," Doug said.

"Not a problem," Chandra agreed, and headed up the stairs, followed by Vivian.

Stephanie, Laura, Denise and Doug filed in and took seats around me. By the confused looks on Laura's and Stephanie's faces, it was clear that Doug hadn't told them he believed I played a role in Harry's suicide.

"So, what now?" I asked.

"We're just following up on our proposal from the night before," Doug said. "Apparently there are others that are trying to get a slice of the pie and we want to make sure you are clear on how many slices you're going to share."

"Ah, a pie analogy," I teased, "I get it. You want to know how I am going to disburse the estate."

"Don't be crass, Bobby," Denise said.

"So, have you mulled this over?" Doug asked.

"Guys, now is not the time for this shit. Dickie is AWOL, a good friend is missing, and a young lady is upstairs making paternity claims regarding Harry. With all this shit going on, you all are down here. Are you kidding me?"

"I'm sorry, Bobby; I'm not a part of this. They told me that they wanted to talk with you regarding Dickie's whereabouts. They never mentioned anything about splitting money. I don't want to have anything to do with this scheme, or whatever it is," Laura said.

"Well, you are saying that because you have already benefited from his generosity," Doug accused.

"That's not fair to single me out like that. It was two hundred bucks. Boy, I made out like a fat rat, didn't I, Bobby?" Laura quipped, and without saying another word, walked out the room and back up the stairs.

"I'm not getting into this now, Doug. I'll figure this thing out when I'm good and ready. And now is not the time. There are too many outsiders in this house for us to be discussing this," I said.

"I don't like what I'm hearing from you, Bobby. Maybe we should pass our suspicions on to Mom and see what she thinks," Doug threatened.

"What type of suspicions?" Stephanie asked. I knew that she was biting at the bit to get some good scandal.

"Remember the gun that Harry killed himself with? Well, Mom took it from him that night and handed it to Bobby. And our brother Bobby gave the gun right back to Harry," Doug accused.

"How convenient for you," Stephanie snapped. "So, you essentially helped Harry pull the trigger."

I laughed. This whole thing was unbelievably ridiculous. "So, now you are joining the mutiny, Stephanie? I can't say that I'm surprised. Listen, all of you need to drop this thing and move on with your business. When the appropriate time comes for me to make decisions about what I want to do with the estate, then I will make those decisions. However, I want to be very clear about one thing – I can do what I want with what Harry left me. It is my decision alone. So, just do me a favor and back the fuck off."

"We'll see what Mom has to say about this," Doug threatened.

"First of all, I really don't care. I'm twenty-five years old and unlike you and Dickie, I quit answering to our mother years ago. So, if you want to be childish and take this to her, that's up to you."

"Bobby, this wasn't our agreement a few days ago," Denise chimed in.

"We had no agreement a few days ago. I simply told you I would mull it over. I've done that and decided to do nothing at the moment."

"Then we'll-" Doug started, but then I interrupted him.

"You won't do anything. You know this whole thing you created is bullshit. The gun will turn up; I guarantee that. I spoke to Jimmy yesterday, and he confirmed that Harry pointed a Colt at him," I said.

"Well, Jimmy's not around to confirm any of this, is he?" Doug smiled.

"What's he talking about, Doug?" Denise asked. "You said that Harry killed himself with the same gun that Bobby gave back to him. Now Bobby is saying it was a different gun."

"Well, the only person that can confirm that is Jimmy," Doug muttered.

"It's all bullshit. Either Doug did something with the Colt when he cleaned Harry's room, or the gun is still missing. This is a weak attempt, driven by greed, to set me up. What I can't believe is that my own brother would stoop this low," I said.

"Wow, Doug, I actually believed you. Bobby wouldn't lie about something like this. I can't believe you would do this," Denise said.

Doug ignored her and turned to me and said, "I don't care what Jimmy told you. You still have an obligation to share with the rest of us."

Doug was beginning to concern me. I could usually count on him to stay out of family controversies. This wasn't his character, so it almost seemed as though someone else was pulling his strings. But it was of no consequence because I wasn't going along with any of what they were proposing.

"Look, meeting is over. I'm not making a decision today. Sorry to disappoint you all," I said.

And then, from upstairs, I heard my mother yell at the top of her lungs. "Oh shit, Mom's getting stirred up again," Stephanie said and ran up the stairs. We all followed.

***

I ran through the kitchen to the living room. When I arrived, my mother was standing in front of Eileen, just inches from her face, screaming at the top of her lungs and calling her all kinds of sluts and whores.

Eleanor and family were sitting quietly by as my mother terrified the young lady. Her companion must have been outside, leaving her to fend for herself.

Doug wedged himself between my mother and Eileen, shielding her from our mother's furious rage. During her interrogation by my mother and Eleanor, the young lady said that Harry had been carrying on with her mother in the late fifties and early sixties, and she was the result of those frequent trysts.

Sarah Foster-Bremen wasn't going to stand by and let someone she didn't know sully the reputation of her dearly departed. I knew my mother was a ticking time bomb and before long, someone or something, besides me, would set her off. Eileen lit the fuse. And my mother exploded.

But Eileen, although showing fear, remained calm and steady amid the storm. The fact that she wasn't backing down concerned me. So, I intervened.

"What evidence do you have that Harry was your father?" I asked.

"He publicly admitted it to me and my mother."

"And your mother can validate this?"

"No, she died a few years ago. But which one of you is Bobby?" she asked.

"That's me. Why do you ask?"

"Because Harry told me that he was leaving everything to you, and that you would take care of me," she proclaimed.

Everyone fell silent.

"This is what he told you?" I asked.

"Yes, his exact words," she answered.

"And when did he tell you this?"

"About a week ago."

"So we are to believe that out of the clear blue sky, Harry visited you and told you this?" I pressed.

"He did. I think he felt guilty that he had ignored me all those years and wanted to make sure that I would be taken care of."

She was good and initially unflappable.

"Okay, so if he what you're saying is true, why didn't he change his will and add you as one of his heirs?" I asked.

"I don't know. This is what he told me. How else would I know that he left everything to you?"

My mother looked at her suspiciously. She wasn't buying the young lady's story at all. And I was certain she wasn't going to believe anything Eileen said.

I was a bit amused by this turn of events, but I also felt Eileen was lying and a scam was in place. We just needed time to connect the dots.

"So, what do you want from us?" I asked her.

"I want my fair share. That's all."

"And how much do you believe is your fair share?" I asked.

"Well, since I am his only known child, I believe that I am entitled to half of the estate."

Eleanor almost fell off the couch. Herbert, who had been dozing off, suddenly was wide awake.

"You little bitch, you need to get the hell out of my house right now," my mother screamed.

"I will, ma'am, but I'm going to get me a lawyer and this will soon be my house."

I intervened at that point and grabbed Eileen by the arm and said, "Look, you need to step outside with me before you get yourself in deeper shit."

She complied and I led her out the front door where I found her companion, sitting on the lawn and smoking a cigarette.

He looked up at me and said, "I'm sorry if we bothered you and your family, but Eileen felt it was the time to stake her claim."

"Stake your claim? Are you kidding me?"

"No, we're not. And your family is going to realize we mean business," he said.

I turned to Eileen. "I don't know who you are, and I certainly have no idea who your boyfriend might be. But your timing really sucks. You show up three days after Harry dies. So, where the hell have you been?"

"He didn't want me to come around," she said, pulled away from me and took a seat in one of the chairs on the porch.

"This whole set up is bullshit, you know that. I don't believe a word of your story. I know you are lying. So what's the scam?" I asked. She seemed a little too uncomfortable with my accusations.

"There's no scam," she stuttered, and glanced over at her boyfriend. "Harry Bremen was my father."

I looked into her eyes. She returned the gaze to study mine. I could tell she was trying to figure her next move "Personally I don't believe you. So, you're going to need a lawyer to prove this."

"And I'll get one," she proclaimed and glanced nervously over at her companion.

Apparently her boyfriend had had enough. He jumped up and walked over to me. "What's all the questioning about anyway? She's Harry Bremen's daughter. And here you are interrogating her like she is some criminal. She was treated badly enough inside the house, by your family."

I was ready to go toe-to-toe with him and said, "First of all, don't come up on me all threatening like that. This is my home, and you are on my property. So, you need to step back and calm down. Secondly, I knew Harry for over half of my life. And during that time, he never spoke of having a daughter or gave any indication that he had a daughter anywhere on the face of this earth."

"Eileen is his daughter, so I guess you're wrong," the man snapped and inched a little closer towards me. I knew that if this resulted in a fight, I would be in for quite a battle. Fortunately, though, despite his current displeasure with me, Doug would still have my back. For us, it was always family first. We settled our differences internally, and would never stand by and allow outsiders to threaten any family member. So Doug would always defend me and I would defend him.

The man moved closer to me. The screen door opened, and Doug stuck his head out. "Is everything all right out here, Bobby?"

When Eileen's boyfriend sized up the situation, he quickly grabbed her by the hand and snapped, "We'll be back for the funeral."

Doug stepped outside and watched them until they turned down a side street and disappeared.

"So what do you think that was all about, Bobby?" he asked.

"I think they probably scanned the obits looking for an easy score and thought we were it. I don't think she has any of Harry's blood flowing through her veins," I answered.

"But how did she know that you inherited everything?"

"I don't know, but I aim to find out."

"I heard him say something about the funeral?"

"Yes, he said they were coming back for the funeral, but I'm not worried about them. I'll call Fred Jackson and let him question them. Maybe that will scare them off."

"Let's hope so because we wouldn't want those slices to get even smaller," he said. He wasn't going to let this go.

***

I headed to my favorite place at the rear of the house. Vivian and Chandra were inside getting ready to leave. We were going to search all of Jimmy's haunts to see if we could sniff him out. When I reached the picnic table, I sat on my familiar perch to relax and take my mind off of everything.

It was nearing eleven in the morning, so we needed to get moving. Today would be one of those days where people came by to visit and offer their condolences. It was important for me to be at home when visitors arrived. And later in the afternoon, my mother would have to go to the funeral home and view the body.

107

"Hey, you," Chandra said, coming up behind me.

"Oh, hey," I answered.

"So, are you mad at me about what I said this morning?"

"No, I'm not mad at all. It was a pretty bizarre accusation, but I guess I understand."

"Well, I am sorry I thought you were gay. I'm glad to hear that you're not upset with me," she said.

"I thought you were convinced that I'm all man based on that moment of pleasure last night." I said. I wasn't sure who did it, but now I was fairly confident it was Chandra.

"What are you talking about, Bobby?" she asked. She seemed a little puzzled.

"Well last night, when... you know..."

"No, I don't know. Last night when I did what?"

"Chandra, you have to know what I'm talking about. Last night when you came over to me when I was asleep on the couch, unzipped my pants, and took care of me."

She looked at me and laughed. "Look, I think you are a nice-looking guy, but I didn't do anything to you last night. Whatever fantasy, real or imagined you had, I wasn't a part of it."

"Don't bullshit me, Chandra. It had to be you. Vivian wouldn't have done that."

"I don't know who did it, but I know I didn't. I don't do that. There's no upside for me."

I wasn't sure if she was kidding with me or sincere. In the day or two that I had come to know Chandra, I couldn't make out if she was telling the truth or not. Her facial expression always seemed to remain fairly fixed when she spoke, showing little emotion during her conversation.

"No idea? Hey, I was sleeping. You came over and unzipped my pants, and did the deed."

"Honestly," Chandra said, halfway smiling, "It wasn't me."

"Well, I guess it must have been Vivian," I conceded. Either it wasn't her or she simply wasn't going to come clean so, I decided to drop it and move on.

"Okay," she smiled. "By the way, you should probably have this."

She reached into her the back pocket of her jeans and pulled out a little, tattered, beige pocket notebook. I recognized it immediately and said, "Where'd you get that?"

"Phillip gave it to me."

I turned red. "That was Harry's. Why the fuck is Phillip snooping around in his things?"

Harry had carried the pocket notebook with him everywhere. Every measurement, phone number or address, or anything important that he needed to remember, he had jotted in the notebook. He never, ever, left the house without it. Apparently, on the day that he killed himself, he must have taken it out of his pocket and put it somewhere.

"Calm down, Bobby, he wasn't snooping around, he…"

"Bullshit. He has no business having this. The only way he could have gotten his hands on this notebook was to search through Harry's things."

"Honestly, he didn't do that. Just hear me out," she implored and tried to take my hand. I jerked away from her and headed for the front door, almost running over Vivian, who was coming in my direction.

"Hey, Bobby, where are you going?" she asked.

I skirted past her and said, "Sorry, Vivian, but I need to settle some business."

Vivian frowned. "What's this all about, Bobby?"

I ignored her and continued inside. I tore into the living room like a raging bull and immediately caught everyone's attention.

Phillip was sitting on the couch between his dad and his uncle Paul. I grabbed him by his shirt and pulled him to his feet.

When I took hold of him, his eyes almost bulged from their sockets. I took my fist, brought it around and caught him with a punch on the chin. Then I jammed my knee into his balls. Phillip slumped to the ground. Before I could get another punch in, I was grabbed from behind by his father, Herbert.

"Leave my son alone," he yelled.

My mom burst from one of the back rooms and came running out. Doug ran up the stairs, from the basement, and slid across the kitchen floor. Eleanor screamed at the top of her lungs just as Chandra came in from outside.

Stephanie ran toward Herbert and grabbed him. "Get your fucking hands off my brother."

Laura and Denise came from the guest bedroom just in time to observe the end of the fray.

"You, fucker," I yelled at Phillip. "You low-life motherfucker."

"Bobby, you stop using that language in this house," my mother yelled at the top of her lungs. "And let go of him."

I was furious. "What gives you the right to go through his things," I yelled as I worked my way out of Herbert's grip and lunged onto Phillip before he could get off the floor. I got in another two punches before Doug grabbed me.

"Bobby, ease off, okay?" he yelled and pulled me away.

Chandra ran across the room and screamed, "What are you doing?"

"I'm taking care of this right now," I said.

"Leave him alone, Bobby. He didn't search through Harry's things," Chandra cried.

"Don't lie for him. I know that he did. Harry wouldn't leave this sitting around."

Chandra whispered in my ear. When it sank in what she had said, I looked down at Phillip and said, "I'm sorry. I made a mistake."

Phillip was trembling. I had no doubt that he could defend himself in a fair fight. But my sucker punches caught him by surprise, and before he could recover, I had nearly pummeled him.

I walked out of the house, ashamed. It wasn't one of my finer moments.

***

Doug followed me outside. I decided to take a walk. I was about fifty yards from the house when Doug caught up with me. The sun was now directly above, and it was getting hot. The humidity, which had lingered for the past few days, promised to hang around for at least another day.

"What was that all about, baby brother?" he asked, finally catching up with me and joining in my walk.

"I made a mistake and attacked Phillip. I just flew off the handle for no reason."

"I know that you're a bit on edge, with this stuff happening and all, but why would you jump him like that?" Doug asked.

"It was a misunderstanding; that's all."

"What kind of misunderstanding could make you lose your cool? You are always the level-headed one in the family. Why did you just fly off the handle like that?"

"Look," I turned to him and grabbed his arm. "I thought he was snooping around in Harry's stuff. A little earlier Chandra gave me his notebook."

"So Harry's mythical notebook emerges. I wondered what happened to it. I think he kept his whole life in that notebook. So you have it now?"

"I do."

"Shit, Bobby, you should have known he didn't mean any harm. After all, he must have given it to Chandra to give to you. So, I don't think he was snooping around."

"I don't know; it just didn't sit well with me that he was in Harry's room looking around."

Doug laughed. "Of course he looked around. Hell, it wouldn't surprise me if all of them looked through the house and stuffed the trunk of their car full of Harry's possessions. You know how these raiding parties work."

I laughed. "You're right about that."

"I always wondered why he protected that book. Maybe he has a map in there to all the money he's probably buried in the back yard," Doug smiled. "Hey look, don't let any of this stuff get you down."

"Yeah, well, I doubt there's anything valuable inside. I'm just glad I have it."

"So what did Chandra say to you that made you stop kicking his ass?"

"She said that her uncle Paul actually found the book and was going to take it, but Phillip thought it was something that I should have and took it from Paul when he fell asleep. It was on the floor of Harry's room. It must have fallen out of his pocket when he, you know...."

"Yeah, I know," Doug nodded. "Well, anyways, you have it now."

"I'm going to forget this happened. But I still sense that these Georgia folk are up to something."

"I don't think it's anything dramatic. They probably just want the house. If they get it, then I'm sure they'll be on their way," he said.

"Have you ever looked in Harry's pocket notebook?" I asked.

"You know he'd never let anyone touch that damn thing. Of course not. Why, is there something in there that I should know about?" Doug asked.

"Not really. The best I can tell it's a bunch of telephone numbers, addresses, and harmless notes," I lied. I hadn't, as of yet, summoned the courage to look through the book. I feared, that inside the book was the answer to why he took his life; and I wasn't ready to face another disappointment.

"Don't you think they have already looked through it before giving it to you?"

"I don't think so. For some reason, I don't believe that Chandra and Phillip really cared what was inside. Uncle Paul, well that's another story. He may have looked through it. But I can't be sure."

"So, if you determine if what's inside the book is not important, are you going to give it to them?"

"Hell, no. I'm not giving them anything that belonged to Harry. Mom can give them some keepsakes, but I won't give them anything," I said.

"Well, in that case, be prepared for a knock-down, drag-out because I don't think they're going to go away that easily. These people seem like the type that won't give up without a fight; especially if they have their sights on something that they want."

"Do they remind you of another family," I laughed.

"Fuck you," Doug smiled.

"Let's get back inside," I suggested and we returned to the house.

***

When I got back, Vivian was thoroughly confused. She had caught the tail end of the situation and didn't know what to make of it.

I walked over to her and asked, "Are you ready to go?"

"Sure, but what was all the commotion about?"

"It was just a misunderstanding I had with Phillip."

"It looked like it was more than a misunderstanding."

"I just flew off the handle. I'm cool, now," I assured her.

"Are you sure you're okay? Let me know if there's something I can do."

"I'm good, Vivian. But I appreciate the offer. Let's get out of here, okay."

"I'm ready whenever you are," she smiled and followed me onto the front porch.

Before we stepped off the porch, I turned to her. "Hey, maybe you can clear something up for me. Last night, when I was sleeping, well, it's hard to say...someone..."

"Gave you a blowjob?"

"Yeah, someone did. Chandra claims it wasn't her."

Vivian laughed. "It had to be her because it wasn't me."

"She says that she didn't do it. And I can't tell if she is lying or not."

"It must have been her, Bobby. I remember last night I fell asleep on the floor right below you, and during the night someone bumped against me. I woke up and saw someone kneeling over you, but it was dark; I was half asleep, so, I know it happened. But it wasn't me, so it had to be her."

"Well, that's what I suspected. But like I said, she claims it wasn't her. She told me that she didn't do it because there's no upside for her."

"Well I agree with her on that. Giving blowjobs is not something I like to do," Vivian laughed.

"When we were dating, you never gave me one."

"And thank God you never asked."

I laughed.

"Maybe we should change the subject. How do you know it was Chandra? Who knows, maybe her mother has a thing for young guys," she teased.

"That is about the most disturbing thought I can imagine. Now it's going to take me the rest of the day to get that image out of my mind."

She laughed along with me for a minute then said, "Worse yet, what if it was one of the old guys. Maybe one of them is in the closet and..."

"Stop it, okay," I said, halfway joking and halfway serious, "Don't even offer that scenario. That's foul."

"Wow, Bobby," she continued with her teasing, "What if one of them came down last night...oh that's just nasty," she laughed.

"It didn't happen, so quit. It was Chandra, and she's just not fessing up to it."

"Okay, if you say Chandra, I'll go along with that."

When we reached the car, Chandra called out to us. "Hey, don't leave without me," she yelled, running toward the car. She jumped in the back seat.

"In light of everything that happened, I didn't think you still wanted to go with me," I said.

"Phillip will be all right. Anyway, I want to see this one-horse town of yours," Chandra said.

"I guess I should have gone in and apologized to him. I shouldn't have lost my head like that."

"He's no worse for the wear. Like I said, he'll be all right. There's no need to apologize." Chandra said and leaned over the seat and tapped Vivian on the back. "Are you okay with me going with you guys? I don't want to intrude."

"It's not a problem, Chandra," she answered.

I turned to Vivian. She was smiling.

Chandra noticed her smile. "Is there something going on that I should know about?"

"Nothing at all. Vivian always smiles at inopportune times."

I could see that Vivian was about to burst into laughter. "Okay, just get it out," I invited, "no need to keep it a secret."

"I can't help it, Bobby," she laughed and turned to Chandra. "I saw someone doing the deed on Bobby last night, and I thought it might have been..."

"Let's just set the record straight right now. It wasn't me. When Bobby told me this morning, I thought it must have been you," Chandra laughed.

"Not me," Vivian declared, with a smile. "So if it wasn't you or me, it must have been a ghost."

"Bobby, maybe you just dreamed the whole thing, and it didn't happen," Chandra suggested.

"Okay, you ladies have had your fun. Let's just drop it, and get out of here."

I pulled the car out of the driveway and headed down the street. I wasn't sure where to go at this point. I just wanted to get away from the house.

I turned to Vivian. "Let's go see if we can find Jimmy."

***

We started our search on the southeast side of town in an area neighborhood known as Columbia Heights. The Heights reminded me of one of those old deserted, Western towns, where only a saloon remained that was patronized by a handful of drunks drinking swill and waiting around for better days and better booze.

Back in the forties, that part of town was the place to be. There was a bar on every corner, speakeasies throughout the neighborhood and illegal gambling establishments in nearly every private home. It was an outlaw area that served the Midwest with pride – being the temporary and preferred stay-over for gangsters and other criminals on their way to such cities as New York, Philadelphia, Cleveland, Chicago and Detroit.

In the early Eighties, though, it was only a shell of its former self, with one remaining bar and many run-down homes in need of razing. Still though, it held on to its criminal legacy. When I was sixteen and got my driver's license it was the one part of town where I could go and purchase beer or wine without worry.

We pulled up in front of the bar, housed in an old, red-bricked building.

"Look," I started, turning to Vivian, "Why don't you and Chandra wait here. I'll go in and see if anyone has seen Jimmy."

Vivian looked out of the window and turned to me. "You don't have to convince me."

"Lock the doors," I said, jumped out of the car and walked into the bar. It was just a few minutes past noon, so the place wasn't too crowded. But still there was a surprisingly decent crowd for this time of day. The establishment wasn't much - a small counter along the wall with about ten tables scattered throughout the room. There was a pool table tucked away in the corner, but it was covered.

I walked over to the bar and sat on one of the stools. I didn't know the bartender by name, but I did recognize him from around town. He came over to me. "What can I get you?" he asked.

"I'm sorry to bother you, but I'm looking for a friend who hangs out here from time to time..."

"Look, we serve drinks here; we don't give information. So officer, why don't you leave and let me get back to my paying customers?"

I expected as much. "I'm not a cop. Seriously, I'm looking for my friend. And he comes here from time to time, and he's disappeared."

"So if you're not a cop, who are you?"

If I wanted information, I had to give him mine. "My name is Bobby," I offered, and continued, "and my friend's name is Jimmy Bushe. Have you seen him?"

"Jimmy comes around often, but I haven't seen him in about a week."

"Okay, I appreciate your help," I said and dropped a ten on the counter and turned to leave.

"Hey," the bartender called as I was about to turn for the door, "if I see him, which Bobby should I say is looking for him?"

I walked back over to the bar. "Tell him Bobby Foster is looking for him."

"Are you related to Dickie Foster?"

"Yeah, he's my brother," I answered. It didn't surprise me that he knew Dickie because everyone seemed to know him.

"Well I'll be damn. Dickie's brother, huh?" He laughed. "Well, I haven't seen Jimmy, but Dickie was in here last night."

I couldn't believe what I was hearing. "You are sure it was Dickie?" I asked.

"Of course I'm sure. Everyone knows Dickie. He was at the table over there. The one closest to the pool table," he pointed.

"Was he by himself?"

"Nope, he was with four dudes and a lady. They were huddled around the table drinking. They left right before closing."

"Did you know any of the people he was with?"

"The men, no, I've never seen them before in my life. It's dark in the bar, so I didn't get a good look at them. But I recognized Dickie. It was good to see him. Oh, and the girl. I know her."

"You do. Who was she?" I asked.

"Her name is Ethel. But she goes by all types of names. She's a heroin addict. I don't know why your brother would be hanging out with the likes of her."

I didn't need to be Sherlock Holmes to figure this one out. "Short, kind of fat chick, with brown hair," I described and added, "Sort of looks like a clown with all the makeup?"

"That sounds like Ethel," he said.

"Thanks. I appreciate your help," I said and left the bar. I was surprised by the turn of events, especially with the new information that Dickie was at the bar with five other people.

I got back into the car and quietly sat down.

"Did anyone have any information on Jimmy?" Vivian asked.

"The bartender says he hasn't been in for nearly a week."

Chandra leaned over the back seat and said, "But you look as though you've seen a ghost."

"No, I haven't, but the bartender has. Two of them."

***

Since we didn't get any information on Jimmy at the bar, we went to his apartment to see if he had turned up. Jackson's investigation the day before was informal – more as a favor for Vivian – and therefore, his place was not a crime scene.

117

I pulled my car into the driveway on the side of the duplex that he was renting. The place wasn't too far from Vivian's house, less than a mile, but was in a particularly run-down area of town. Vivian and Chandra decided to accompany me inside.

We stepped onto the porch and knocked on the door. Predictably, there was no answer. Vivian stepped around me and turned the door knob. The door was unlocked.

"That doesn't mean anything," Vivian said as she pushed the door open. "Jimmy never locked his place."

When we entered, we stepped inside of a hallway. To our right were stairs to the second floor, to our left, presumably the living room and straight ahead, at the end of the hall, the kitchen.

The house was in shambles. There were clothes, property and furniture strewn throughout the first floor hallway and living room. Vivian called out Jimmy's name a couple of times.

Chandra grabbed my arm and moved as close to me as she could. The house, in its present condition, was in a frightening state.

I slowly moved down the hall to the kitchen. Surprisingly, unlike that rest of the first floor, it was quite clean, the dishes neatly stacked in a strainer on the sink. There was a teapot on the stove. I walked over to it and placed my hand on it.

"It's still warm, ladies. Someone has been here recently."

Chandra looked alarmed. "Do you think we're safe?"

"Let's check upstairs," Vivian suggested.

"I'm sure we are okay. Apparently, whoever used the tea kettle felt at home doing so. Maybe Jimmy came through here earlier," I said.

Vivian whispered in my ear, "Jimmy drinks coffee not tea."

"Well that's comforting to know. Okay then, let's go check the upstairs. But stay close behind me, okay?" I advised.

I hated walking into the unknown. I was nervous but wanted to put up a strong front for the ladies. I moved carefully and slowly up the stairs. The women were so close to me that if I made a sudden move, I would send them tumbling back down the stairs.

"How many rooms are upstairs?" I asked Vivian.

She leaned close and whispered in my ear, "Three."

I assumed two bedrooms and a bathroom. At the very top of the stairs was the master bedroom. I looked inside and other than clothes thrown over a mattress that was on the floor, there was nothing suspicious.

We continued down the hallway to the guest bedroom, which was the next door to our right. However, as we neared the bedroom's door, we heard the sound of the water running, coming from the bathroom. It sounded as if someone was taking a shower. I looked back at Vivian and Chandra, who were both petrified. Then I scanned the hallway for some object that I could grab and use as a weapon. Sitting next to the stairs, in a small vase, was an umbrella. I grabbed it and told the women to go back downstairs.

"Bullshit," Vivian said, "We're staying with you."

The bathroom was the last door on the right. The door was partially cracked. I crept up to the door and waited. I was shaking. Even during my military police days a situation like this one made me nervous.

A few moments after I had stationed myself in front of the door, the shower was turned off . As I waited, I realized that this really wasn't a sensible thing to do. But, I persisted and took a deep breath and kicked the door all the way open and charged into the bathroom with the umbrella. As soon as I stepped through the door the umbrella somehow slipped and popped open.

I was fortunate that it did because a startled, older gray-haired, stark naked, stocky gentleman stood in front of me. He dropped his towel and put his hands up.

"Who the hell are you?" he yelled.

"Who are you?" Vivian screamed, moving around me.

"I'm Brad Bushe."

"Brad Bushe?" Vivian questioned.

I caught it right away. He was Jimmy's dad. The one that Jimmy told me he would kill if he ever saw him again. "You're Jimmy's old man, aren't you?"

He picked the towel up and covered himself. "Excuse me," he said, walking past me and to the guest bedroom. "Yes, I am. And if you are looking for Jimmy, I haven't seen him. I got here early this morning. Jimmy hasn't been around, but he always told me that he kept a spare key under an old tire in the back yard. I used that to get in."

"I'm Vivian," she introduced as Brad Bushe went into the spare bedroom.

"Nice to meet you, Vivian," he said, and before he closed the door, added, "should that mean something to me?"

Before anyone could answer, he slammed the door shut. I was pissed that he had treated Vivian so rudely and was determined to bring it up with him when he got dressed.

We waited for Bushe for about ten minutes. I was getting tired but kept in mind that he was an old man, and it may take him a little longer.

After few more minutes, I got tired of waiting and knocked on the door. He didn't answer, so I knocked again. Still, there was no answer, so I tried the door, but it was locked.

"Shit," I cursed, and turned to the ladies. "Let's get downstairs," I said and ran toward the first floor.

When we reached the ground floor, we ran through the front door and to guest bedroom side of the house. Sure enough, the window was opened and it looked as though this mystery person had exited the room down the short fire escape.

"Fuck," I muttered. "Wait here," I told the ladies. I climbed up the fire escape to the open window and entered the room. It was clean. The bag that I had seen on the bed was gone.

I left the room, climbed back down the fire escape, and headed for the car.

"So what do we do now?" Vivian asked.

"I'm not sure. But remember yesterday, when you came by and said that Jackson had seen blood in the kitchen?"

"Yes, that's what he told me," Vivian answered.

"So then, where was this blood? You think maybe the old guy had something to do with Jimmy's disappearance and cleaned up the place to cover his tracks?"

"You think his father would harm him?" Vivian asked.

"Nowadays you never know. Stranger things have happened."

"So what's our next move?" Vivian asked. She somehow seemed better today, and less concerned about Jimmy. I got the impression that she was growing tired of looking.

"Well, if a crime was committed, then I believe Jackson is on top of it. He canvassed the house yesterday, so I suspect if he found something he's following up. So, really, there's nothing more that we can do. Anyways, I need to get home, Vivian. Are you spending the night at my house or at yours?"

"My mother came back today. Just drop me off there. I'll come around tomorrow and pick up my car. If I don't hear anything maybe we can go out tomorrow to look for him," she suggested.

"I don't know. I think looking for him may be a waste of time. Knowing Jimmy, he is hiding out. If he's involved in something, I don't expect that he will turn up anytime soon. He'll wait for the coast to clear."

"I'm sure you're right, Bobby. Anyway, thanks for taking me out to look for him. By the way, what did you mean when you said that the bartender saw a ghost?"

I waited for Chandra, who was walking ahead of us, to get into the car. "Dickie's missing, too. No one in the family has heard from him. But the bartender said that he saw Dickie yesterday at the bar with a group of people."

"It's strange that both Jimmy and Dickie are missing. Do you think the two are related?"

"At first I thought so, but now I'm beginning to think Dickie's disappearance is not a disappearance at all."

"You think he is just kind of hiding out from the family?" She asked.

"I'm not sure. But I intend to find out," I answered. We got into the car and left.

*****

When I returned home cars were crammed everywhere in front of our house, along the street. Some cars were even parked next to Vivian's car on the front lawn. I had to park down the street from the house.

"What do you suppose this is all about?" Chandra asked, while we made the short walk from the car to the front porch.

"I don't know. I expect some folk stopped by to pay their respects. But you normally don't see a crowd like this until after the funeral."

We stepped inside to a house full of guests, milling around and making small talk. I carefully weaved my way through the crowd, nodding a greeting here and there to a few people whom I recognized, until I located my mother in the kitchen. I moved over to her. She was sitting at the head of the table – her usual seat – talking with some people around her.

I positioned myself next to her and whispered into her ear, "Where did all these people come from?"

She smiled and excused herself from a conversation she was having with the folk around her. She turned to me. "Have you seen or heard from your brother?" she asked, ignoring my question.

"No I haven't," I answered.

"Then you need to find him, tonight," she snapped and went back to her conversation. My mom was on edge, and I didn't believe it was due to the upcoming funeral or anything surrounding Harry's death. This was all about Dickie.

The door leading to the basement was just behind my mother. I carefully made my way around her chair and headed down the stairs, only to be greeted by a basement full of people. They were everywhere. I spied my sister Laura standing in a corner and talking with some guy. She looked as though she needed to be rescued, so I went over to her and took her hand.

"Hey Sis, I need to see you out back. Please excuse us," I said to the guy standing next to her, and led Laura out through the sliding glass doors into the back yard. Oddly, despite all the people inside the house, no one was outdoors. I took a seat on my favorite picnic table. She sat next to me.

"Thanks for that," she said. "That guy was really weird. He claims he went to school with me, but I don't recall ever seeing him in my life."

I laughed. "He's probably been stalking you for most of your college years, and you just didn't know it."

She playfully punched me in the arm. "Stop that. It's not funny."

"What's with all the people?" I asked.

"When we came home from the funeral home, Mom got a call from one of her church lady friends and the next thing I know, cars are pulling in front of the house like crazy. People were getting out, bringing food in. Bobby, it's been non-stop. By the way, Mama is pissed at you."

"Why?"

"She thought that maybe you were coming down to the funeral home."

"I thought so too, but I couldn't make it. I was busy looking for Jimmy."

Laura laughed. "Well, Mom is a little pissed about that, as well. She's wasn't pleased to hear that you were out and about with two women looking for Jimmy when you should have been looking for your brother. At least, that's the way she put it."

"Of course. She loves her Dickie," I smiled.

"That's for sure. Life is not right unless she hears from him."

The sliding door opened, and Fred Jackson stepped outside into the evening air. It was starting to get a little dark, so he didn't notice us right away. He reached in his pocket and pulled out a cigarette and lighter. When he lifted his head after lighting his cigarette, he saw us.

"You scared me," he laughed, taking a drag on his cigarette. "You should never surprise a cop."

"You're not in uniform. So it doesn't count," I joked.

He walked over to us. "Hi, Laura. I understand congratulations are in order."

"Thank you, Freddie. I'm glad I finally managed to get through my four years."

"I can imagine that can be difficult. I know this may sound inappropriate in light of the present circumstances, but you should still be acknowledged for that tremendous accomplishment."

Laura smiled and said, "Again, thanks. It was tough but I'm on to other things now."

I could tell that Laura was becoming uncomfortable with Freddie's conversation. He was one of those creepy guys that preyed on younger women. I didn't want him to even think that any of my sisters were in play. So, I quickly changed the conversation and said, "I stopped by Jimmy's today but there was no sign of him. A guy was staying in his house that said he was Brad Bushe, Jimmy's father."

"Brad Bushe, huh?" Jackson started, and took another drag from his cigarette. "I went to school with Brad Bushe. That's Jimmy's uncle, not his father. As far as I know, Jimmy's father is dead. Anyway, it doesn't matter. Jimmy's not classified as a missing person."

"But no one has seen him since the other night. So how could he not be a missing person? And the blood at his place - isn't that kind of strange?"

Jackson blew the smoke through his nose and mouth and dropped the cigarette onto the ground and extinguished it. "The forensic team thinks the blood is some type of animal blood. We believe the house was in shambles because Jimmy is a slob. But none of that matters anyway. He's not missing."

"Why is that?"

"Because, I was out at the Smart Bar last night, and I saw him there, having a drink."

"You saw Jimmy last night?"

"Yes, I sure did. And he was sitting at a table with your brother, Dickie."

***

Jackson didn't have much more to tell us regarding Dickie and Jimmy. He explained that he saw them at the club, but before he got around to speaking to them, they had left.

I thought it was strange that Jackson had seen them together in the neighboring city. It only seemed to cloud the mystery even more. So, when Jackson left, I realized that I had more questions than answers.

The crowd began to dwindle inside the house. People were finally starting to leave. Most of the folk that came knew my mother through the church, so in a few hours, Sunday morning, they would all see each other again.

I walked through the house with a plastic bag picking up paper plates and cups left by the guests. In the kitchen, food, mostly desserts, were everywhere.

My mother had already retired to her room. After the guests had left, she didn't have anything to say to me. And while there were still a few people lingering around, they were talking to my sisters, so I guess Mom felt she didn't need to stay and entertain them.

Chandra came over to me as I was picking up the living room. "Interesting day, huh?"

"Certainly was, and unfortunately, it's not over yet."

"How do you mean?"

"The way things have been going; anything is liable to happen in the next two or three hours."

Fred Jackson's revelation had shocked me. I wasn't sure of what kind of game Dickie was playing, but too many people were seeing him around town. So, I had no choice but to conclude that he left on his own free will. What I couldn't figure out was what he was actually up to and why he was avoiding contact with the family.

The Jimmy part was interesting as well. It was all so very strange and quite frankly, gave me a headache just thinking about it.

"Why don't you take a break from this cleaning and go for an evening walk with me. I need to get out of here and get a little air," Chandra said.

It wasn't a bad suggestion. The heat during the day, coupled with the humidity had been nearly oppressive. The house, though a mess, could wait. And, it looked as though no one else in my family – or now extended family – was interested in picking the place up.

"You're right. I need to get out of here and get some air, too. The cleaning can wait."

Most of the family, including Eleanor, Phillip, Herbert and Paul were downstairs going through photo albums. My mother had told them to take what remembrances they wanted. So, I dropped the black plastic garbage sack in the middle of the floor and headed for the door.

It was a beautiful night. I could actually see the stars, so I knew that cooler temperatures were on the way.

We walked across the grass, turned left on the street and began our trek north, away from the house. It was a fairly quiet evening and only interrupted occasionally by a lone car rumbling down the street. Our short journey had begun in quiet, but it wasn't long before Chandra broke the silence.

She took my left hand and said, "A penny for your thoughts."

"Chandra, my mind is so full of shit right now that it's about ready to explode. My brother and friend are missing. The funeral is Monday. My mom and siblings are pissed at me. A long-lost daughter entered the scene. I mean what next? It seems that each day brings a different surprise."

"I'm here to offer my support in any way possible," she said.

"I appreciate that. But erasing all the things that have happened the last few days from my mind, is going to be extremely difficult."

"You shouldn't ever try to forget the past, just learn from it. You may never erase it."

I understood where Chandra was coming from but I didn't think that I would ever be able to accept any of this. "I just need to come to terms with everything that has happened and then move on."

"What about your brother," she said, as we turned and headed west down an alley. There was a small playground at the end of the alley, and I thought we could sit there and relax for a few minutes.

"I don't know. Dickie is Dickie. I have no idea where he is at. My mom is insistent that I find him as though his disappearance is somehow my responsibility. I don't know what to do about it. I'm just hoping that he'll turn up soon."

We arrived at the playground, and Chandra went over and sat on one of the swings. "Push me."

I stepped behind her and gave her a slight shove. "Harder. I want to go higher," she squealed with the delight of a small child.

I pushed her harder and continued to push her as she went up and

"Come in," Chandra's voice invited. I opened the door and walked into the room.

Chandra was lying on the bed, stark naked, with her head propped up by a pillow. "I thought you would enjoy waking up to a surprise," she smiled.

I smiled and thought about jumping into the sack with her, but my common sense kicked in before things could get out of control. "As much as I want to jump on this bed with you, Chandra, I'm not going to do it."

She laughed. "Aw, Bobby, why not? It's just us and I really enjoyed last night."

"Chandra, you're lying naked in my mother's bed. The woman is like a blood-hound. As soon as she walks in the door, she is going to smell this in the air. No, sweetheart, no Bobby for you."

"Fine," she smiled, jumped off the bed. When I saw her jump off the bed, I almost changed my mind. In fact, I wanted to tell her to get back on the bed and jump off two or three more times.

Chandra grabbed her panties, a button-up blouse and put them on. It was still difficult to concentrate, but at least it was manageable. "Why didn't you go to church?" I asked.

"I could ask you the same thing," she started. "I was tired, for obvious reasons."

I didn't think our little roll in the park the night before was enough to fatigue her, but I played along. "Oh, so that tired you out last night?"

"Yes," she said, walked over to me and gave me a kiss. "That was the best sixty seconds I have ever had."

I laughed. "Wow, belly shot, huh? Well, I thoroughly enjoyed myself even if it was only short-lived. I'm hoping we may be able to revisit that opportunity...but," I caught her before she could say anything, "at a more appropriate time and place."

"You really take the fun out of everything, don't you, Bobby," she said and playfully punched me.

"Follow me to the kitchen and I'll make you a cup of coffee. Maybe that will get your mind off of sex," I offered.

I went to the kitchen and turned on the burner and placed the coffee pot on the stove. "We only have instant coffee. I hope that works for you."

"Instant is fine," Chandra smiled and took a seat at the table.

I sat down next to her while the water heated up. "So, what are you going to do today?" I asked her.

"Well, I was hoping to screw your brains out, but apparently you have decided to take the fun out of this new relationship."

"Harsh, Chandra. Very harsh. I want you so badly right now. Believe me; I'm doing everything that I can to stop myself from jumping on you," I said just as my shorts bulged.

Chandra laughed. "I see you're ready."

"You're hard to resist." I sat in one of the chairs at the kitchen table, and before I could fully settle in my seat, she unexpectedly slid out of her chair and quickly straddled me, in mine.

She put her arms around me. "Come on. Let's have a little fun," she urged. She rocked slowly in my lap. I didn't stop her. I wanted to take the high road, to be the bigger person in Harry's house and honor his memory appropriately. But I was young and horny - with an erection. And those facts alone superseded any rational thoughts or common sense that my sex-crazed mind could muster.

I surrendered and leaned against the back of the chair. I closed my eyes and enjoyed the next few moments, drifting away in pleasure. But when common sense finally caught up with my brain, it was too late. "Chandra, I can't hold it in. We need to stop."

But she didn't and I couldn't pull away. Finally it was too late.

"Did you-" she started.

"Yes," I answered and added, "God damn, I should have taken it out." I had done a very stupid thing. The night before, I had used a condom.

"It's okay. I won't get pregnant. I'll go take care of that right now," she said.

"How are you going to do that, Chandra? I can't reverse what I just did."

"Don't worry, we have our ways," she smiled and left the room.

"Shit," I screamed and slammed my hand on the table. The telephone rang. I pulled my shorts and pants up and walked over to it, still angry with myself and answered it.

"Hello," I growled.

"Bobby." I immediately recognized Dickie's voice.

"Dickie, where the hell are you? Mama is driving me crazy asking about your whereabouts." Of course he would be a coward and call while our mother was at church.

"I'm okay. Listen, I don't have time to chat. I need you to meet me tonight, around 10:00, at the mall. Can you do that?"

"Dickie, what the hell is going on?" I asked.

"Look, I don't have time for this shit. Can you meet me or not?"

"Yeah, but the funeral is tomorrow, so I can't be fooling around with you too long."

"You won't be. I just need a ride."

"Where do you want me to pick you up?"

"I'll be in the mall parking lot, on the back side. Just be there at 10:00, okay?"

"I'll be there." It all sounded a little suspicious to me – picking him up on the back side of the mall. Whatever he was involved in couldn't be good. I needed to keep my eyes opened and stay on the alert.

"See you at 10:00," he muttered and ended the call.

Chandra re-emerged from the back. Apparently, whatever precautions she was to take, she had taken because now she was fully dressed. I was still pissed at myself for being so careless. The last thing I needed was for that to happen.

She walked over to me and gave me a kiss. "You look worried."

"I didn't mean for that to play out the way it did. That was careless of me."

"Don't let it worry you," she said, and rubbed my hair with her hand.

"I'm not ready for accidents, Chandra. I have some more living to do before I become a dad."

She smiled. "I've taken care of it, so put it out your mind. Besides," she laughed, "if it happens, it happens. You'll be a great dad."

It was clear that Chandra was no different than anyone else in the house. She had an agenda as well.

***

The holy rollers piled back into the house a few minutes after one o'clock. They looked hot, drained, and exhausted. It seemed to me the purpose of church on a Sunday was to reinvigorate and renew - to get some motivation and inspiration at the end of the week to allow one to start a new week with vim and vigor. But since I had basically excommunicated myself from the church, I didn't level any criticism toward the devout.

Shortly after they had returned home, my mother approached me and said, "We need to talk about this car situation."

I knew I couldn't avoid having this conversation forever. Stephanie was a relentlessly spoiled bitch. And she was a coward. Her courage came from alcohol – without it, she was docile, compliant, and non-confrontational. Yet when she became liquored up, she discovered her courage. When sober, she avoided confrontation, and had our mother do her bidding.

I sat on the couch. "Sure, what about the car?" I asked. As soon as the last word left my mouth, I saw the door to the guest bedroom slightly cracked open. I assumed Stephanie was listening.

"With tomorrow being Harry's funeral, and people leaving, we need to know if you are going to give the green car to Stephanie."

"I haven't decided yet," I said. Truthfully, at that point I hadn't decided what to do with anything. Mother wasn't happy with my answer. She frowned.

"I'm disappointed to hear this," she said. "If Stephanie doesn't know if she'll get the car today, she has to call her boyfriend to come pick Tanya and her up tomorrow, after the funeral."

"So, he needs to spend more time with his daughter," I said.

"The least amount of time Trent spends here, the better. I can't believe you would push your sister off on him."

"Trent's not my problem, Mama. That's Stephanie's deal. She got back with him against your advice. So she can live with it. It won't hurt him to drive up here and pick her up."

I knew that my mother was just seconds away from exploding. But she somehow managed to maintain her posture. Well almost.

She walked over to me and whispered in my ear, "I can't believe a son of mine would be so damn selfish. I should have drowned you in the river when you were born."

I stood there, speechless, as she walked away.

***

I pulled into Vivian's driveway. I managed to escape the house without any passengers. I just needed some time away from my family.

Vivian's mother answered the door. She seemed to be excited to see me. Mrs. Mathis was always consistent in that regard. During the entire time I dated her daughter she always treated me with kindness.

"Hi, Bobby," she said, stepping aside to let me into the house.

"Good afternoon, Mrs. Mathis. Beautiful day," I greeted and stepped into the hallway.

"Yes, it is. You know that I will be at the funeral tomorrow, but the mister, he has to work."

I didn't expect old man Mathis to be there. And honestly, I guessed he wouldn't be working either. He was antisocial.

"Thank you, Mrs. Mathis. I appreciate your concern. Is Vivian here?"

"Yes, she's out back sitting on the porch. I'm surprised she didn't hear your car when you pulled up."

"Thank you, ma'am," I said, and walked through the kitchen to their back porch. Vivian was sitting on a swing gently rocking.

I took a seat on the swing, next to her, but she didn't seem to notice. The temperature was beginning to cool a bit, and a nice breeze had stirred and found its way through the screened-in porch. When the breeze hit us, Vivian gently rested her head on my shoulder.

"He's not coming back, Bobby," she whispered.

"He may come back. Don't give up on Jimmy."

She inhaled deeply and then exhaled. "Last summer, when you and I were together, sitting on the back porch with you was the best time of my life."

I chuckled softly. "Then my dear, you have had a rather uneventful life."

She punched me on the thigh. "Why are you here, Bobby?"

"Because right now, Vivian, you are the only real person in my life. Everyone else seems to have a personal agenda or motive. I just needed some sanity."

"That's very sweet of you. This Chandra, she has her eyes on you. You should be careful with her," she unexpectedly warned.

I thought maybe Vivian was a little jealous. "She's okay."

"Bobby, she's on a husband hunt. And the way she looked at you the other day, well, I think she has you locked squarely in her sights. Be careful with this one or you may be saying 'I do' in nine months."

Vivian could see right through me. "How did you know?"

"You're not hard to read when you feel guilty about something you've done. I figured it wouldn't be long before you two found your way into the sack."

"Yes, I made that mistake twice."

Vivian laughed. "Busy man. Twice since I last saw you?"

"Yes. Twice. Last night and this morning." I felt a bit embarrassed talking about this with her.

"So now you come to me after rolling in the hay with her? I don't get it."

"I think maybe I've come to the same conclusion as you. That she's looking for a husband. I just needed to get away from her and talk to you."

"I hope you used some type of protection."

I blushed. She looked up at me and caught me right away.

"Bobby, you didn't?"

"I did the first time, but the second time, well, unfortunately I didn't."

"You better pray she doesn't get pregnant. She's not the type to go away easily. She'll have the baby and hook you into marrying her."

"How could you possibly know this? I mean, you were only with her for a day."

"You're so naïve, Bobby. Anyways, women know these things," she

134

smiled, and gave me a kiss on the cheek.

"Where would I be without your advice," I kidded.

"A married man with about three kids running around," Vivian laughed.

"So, we're still friends?"

"Bobby, you and I will always be friends. I can't imagine living my life without you being a part of it. I'll never forget you."

That caught me by surprise. "Did I miss something? You sound as though you are going somewhere."

Vivian laughed. "Bobby, you were always a bit slow on the uptake. This is why you need me in your life." She stood up from the swing and walked over to the edge of the porch and leaned on the rail and looked over the backyard.

"In September, I'm moving from Ohio to California. My brother lives in Oxnard. He says he can help me get into UC Santa Barbara."

"Wow, that's shocking. You're moving all the way to California? I didn't see this happening."

"I decided to move a month or two ago. I knew this thing with Jimmy wasn't going anywhere. And this town, well, it's dragging me under. Bobby, I don't want to end up in this town, with only football every Friday night, the start of bowling league and a bunch of dirty diapers to look forward to. That's not for me. Hey, you should come with me."

I laughed. "As appealing as that offer sounds, if I accepted, the only reason I would be going to California is to hang out with you. Other than you, there wouldn't be anything in California that appeals to me."

"What's so bad about wanting to hang out with me? Hanging out with you sounds really nice. And besides, you would rather have this place than California?"

"No, Vivian. This town isn't my future. Neither is California. I don't know where I supposed to be, but I'm sure I'll figure it out soon."

Vivian walked over to me and gave me a hug. She hugged me tightly. When I tried to pull away, she held on longer. She whispered in my ear, "Jimmy's dead."

I wanted to push away to ask her how she had come to this conclusion, since there was no news of Jimmy. But honestly, that moment, that time, was exactly what I needed.

And I think she sensed that I was looking for an explanation. She leaned close to my ear once and simply whispered, "A woman knows these things."

***

When I returned to the house, Chandra met me at the door. "We need to talk," she said, before I could take a step inside.

I didn't' know what to make of this, so I followed her to the rear of the house and took a seat next to her on my familiar perch on the picnic table.

"So, what's up?" I asked.

"Me and you," she said.

So, I thought, *here comes her angle.* Vivian did a fairly decent job of opening my eyes in regard to Chandra. And of course, my mind kept analyzing the entire situation, and each time it returned the same results; this wasn't a relationship I wanted or should pursue. So I felt it best just to break it off before it even got started. "As far as I'm concerned, there is no you and I," I said, rather coldly. Chandra looked like a boxer who had been dazed by a punch.

"I'm surprised to hear that, Bobby. So there's no us, huh? What about last night and what about this morning?"

"We made a mistake, Chandra. We had sex. But that's really all we had. Other than that, there's nothing between us," I said. I could see that she was getting a little angry.

"Well, I just don't understand this," she said.

"I'm sorry, Chandra, if I gave you the indication that I wanted a relationship. That wasn't my intent. We're all going through a very difficult time right now and emotions get mixed, and then this or that happens, and you know..."

"No, Bobby, I don't know. We slept together. To me, that is a very special thing. I just don't give my body to anyone."

"I'm sorry. I guess I misread the signals."

136

She grimaced angrily. "Well, believe me; if something should come of this, I am going to press the issue."

"Okay, I see the game. Threaten me with paternity? You know what, that's bullshit. You're too smart to get pregnant. So, why don't you tell me, Chandra, what you really want? Why don't you just put it all on the table? I'm tired of you walking around here as though you have no personal agenda. Every fucking person in this house has their own agenda. And it somehow involves what I have."

I think my observations caught her by surprise. She stammered for a minute then said, "Well, I want what rightfully belongs to my family."

I laughed. Then it became crystal clear. "So, it was you the other night."

"Yes, it was me. I'll do what I have to do for my family."

"So, you gave me a blow job and fucked me for a house? That's one expensive piece of ass."

"Bobby, it doesn't have to be like this. You are a great guy. I think we could probably-"

"There's no way in hell that I'm going to get with you, Chandra. You have a price, just like everyone else. So, yes, it has to be exactly like this. You need to move on, Chandra. There is no way that we are going to get together."

"So what about the house?"

"What's so special about that damn house? It's just a house and from what I can gather from the paperwork, not all that impressive."

"It's our house, Bobby," Chandra screamed. "Harry stole it from us, just like you are stealing it from your mother."

I wasn't interested in hearing any more. "Look, Chandra, you need to back the fuck off before I get angry. As for the house, I haven't made a decision about it yet. But I will, and when I do, you will be one of the first to know."

I heard someone call Chandra's name. I looked around to the side of the house and saw her Uncle Paul walking down the hill toward us. I turned back to Chandra.

"What's this all about?" I asked.

"I don't know," she said, and turned to her uncle. "Uncle Paul, Bobby and I are chatting."

"I need to talk to the young man," he snapped, walking my way. I could see that he looked a bit confrontational, and I didn't care. *Honest to Go*, I thought, *I will drop this fucker where he stands if he tries any shit*. While I loved and respected his brother Harry, I didn't give a shit about Paul.

"I don't have anything to say to you," I answered, turning back to Chandra.

"Well, I have to talk to you," he insisted and made his way to us. We were on the side of the house, below the side kitchen window. If things got out of control, hopefully someone in the kitchen would hear us.

He grabbed my arm and attempted to pull me around to face him. "You have something that I want."

"Take your hands off me," I said, and pulled out of his grip.

He moved toward me again. "Uncle Paul, let's not make a scene," Chandra suggested.

Paul backed down. "You should thank my niece. She saved your ass," he boasted.

Paul didn't worry me. Unless he had a gun - which was a very real possibility - he wasn't going to take me. "Look, I don't know what the deal is with your family, but if you keep this shit up, all of you are going to have to leave right away."

"I don't think your mother minds us being here. Right now, she's in the kitchen with my sister preparing a dinner for everyone," Paul said.

"Good for the both of them. I hope they are very happy together in their new life as friends. But for now, you need to back off."

"I need my brother's notebook. I want you to give it to me or else," Paul threatened.

"You had the notebook. Your own people gave it to me. I'm not giving it back to you."

"Please, give me the notebook. I need it."

"What's in this notebook that is so damn important?"

"That doesn't concern you. I need it. My brother would want me to have it."

138

He began to calm down. In fact, his face, instead of anger, wore a sad expression. It just seemed as though the hostility between us dissipated.

"Can you tell me why this is so important to you, please, and maybe I will consider handing it over to you."

"It's just my brother's book. I should have it; that's all. I don't have anything to remember him by. There's nothing special in the book. But everything is written in his hand. So, when I touch this book, I'll remember him. When I see his poorly scrawled handwriting on the notebook pages, I will think of my brother, Harry. That's the only reason I want it."

I looked at Chandra. "If this is the case, why didn't you just let him keep it when he found it?"

"It wouldn't have been proper. You can't just come into a house and take things that don't belong to you," she explained.

I really wasn't convinced of their sincerity. "Let me think about it, and I'll let you know tomorrow."

Paul reddened and started to speak but couldn't get his words out.

Chandra ran over to me. "Please, Bobby, can't you be decent and just give him the book?"

They were trying to scam me. Something in the notebook must have value. I figured that when Phillip took the notebook from Paul, he didn't know that and innocently handed it over. But now I believed Paul had convinced them otherwise.

Paul's anger returned. "Okay, just let me know," he ended, and walked away, in a huff.

Chandra looked at me. "Why can't you just give it to him? It has no value to you."

"I said that I would think about it. Give me a day to mull it over and look through the book. If I'm satisfied, then I'll give the book to Paul."

"Well, I think you are being hard-headed about this. To me, there isn't any reason that you should keep this book. My uncle just wants a small part of Harry's life to remember him by. This book was something that he apparently carried every day. There is no logical reason why Uncle Paul should not have it."

"Chandra, if you or anyone in your family is not happy with my time line, then, quite frankly; you all can kiss my ass."

I didn't know where my animosity was coming from, but as I stood there and talked, I just seemed to get angrier and more suspicious. They were up to something.

Chandra made two fists and looked as though she was going to attempt to strike out at me. But she dropped her defensive posture and ran inside, crying.

***

I had no idea why Dickie wanted to meet in a deserted parking area. All the stores had closed an hour before and there wasn't a single car left in the parking lot. The rear of the mall bordered train tracks that separated the mall parking from an expansive corn field.

The lighting wasn't very good, with only a little illumination coming from the few poles scattered about the lot. I wasn't happy with the setup.

Doug had wanted to come with me, but I thought he should stay behind. Dickie was acting strange. Too many people might scare him off. This was something I didn't want because I wanted to see this entire mess resolved. Dickie needed to be at home, safely in the overprotective arms of our loving mother so the two of them could live happily ever after.

I pulled the green Chrysler under a single light pole and turned the car off. I got out of the car and looked around the empty parking lot. No one was in sight.

There was sufficient light in the parking lot where I could see if someone walked up on me, but not enough to see a face until they were on top of me. I scanned my surroundings, carefully squinting to see if I could make out anything. However, it was perfectly still.

I sat on the hood of the car and remained alert. As I scanned the rear of the parking lot, toward the train tracks, I saw someone steal into view, from out of a cornfield. The person crossed the tracks, stepped into the parking lot, and then walked quickly toward me. I couldn't make out his face but from his posture, body build and walk, I was sure that it was Dickie.

He was slightly hunched over as he neared and seemed to be nervously looking around the parking area. Dickie covered the distance from the tracks to my location quickly, and in a few short minutes was standing in front of me.

"Bobby," he said in a dry, cracking voice. He looked behind him and then nervously turned back toward me.

"Hey, Dickie, what's up man?" I anxiously asked.

"Nothing. Look, I need you to do me a favor."

"So that's it. No one in the family has seen you in a couple of days and all you have to say is that you need a favor? No explanation or anything. What gives, man?"

"Bobby, I don't have time for this. There are people looking for me, and I need your help. I'll explain when the time is right. Right now though, I need you to sign something."

"Sign something? Dickie, I'm not signing anything."

He grabbed me by the front of my neck. His hand was like a vice-grip on my throat. "God damn it, Bobby, shut the fuck up for a minute and hear me out."

"Shit, Dickie, okay," I said when he released his grip. "Fuck, what's so damn important that you have to have my signature tonight?"

"This," he said, shoving a document in front of me. I took it from him.

"So what kind of document is it?" I asked.

"Just sign it, okay," he insisted.

I laughed. "I'm not signing this. For one, I have no idea what it is. Secondly, I can smell a scam."

Dickie unexpectedly backhanded me. I dropped the paperwork on the ground and tried to regain my senses. My cheek throbbed. "Stop it, Dickie."

He hit me again. This time, I lost my footing and fell to the asphalt. Then I took a sharp kick to the stomach. I curled over and almost vomited. I tried to speak, but before I could get a word out he came down on the back of my head with a fist. I collapsed and lay prone on the parking lot.

I was in so much pain, I was nearly senseless. It seemed that every part of my body ached. Dickie paced around me as I remained face down on the cold asphalt. He was mumbling something, but I couldn't make any sense out of it.

I heard another voice. Someone yelled something to Dickie.

"He won't sign it," I heard Dickie say, and then, I took a kick to the head and passed out.

***

I regained consciousness a few minutes before midnight. I focused my eyes and saw my brother, Doug, standing over me. Someone had put a compress on my head. I jumped up. But when I did, my head hurt so badly, I quickly fell back.

"Whoa, slow down," Doug advised.

"Where's Dickie?" I asked.

"We haven't seen Dickie," Doug answered. Despite the pain, I managed to work my way into a sitting position but then I felt faint. I fell back onto the couch. Doug reached down and caught me and gently helped me.

"Just lay down, Bobby," he advised.

My mother came over to me. "Are you all right, Bobby?" she asked and took a seat in the chair next to the couch.

"No, I'm not all right, Mama. I hurt all over, and it was Dickie who did this to me," I said. My head was throbbing. It felt as though someone had smacked me with a baseball bat.

Mom glared at me. "Your brother wouldn't do such a thing," she said firmly.

I ignored my mother. It didn't surprise me that she was standing firmly behind her saintly son. I turned to Doug. "How did I get here?"

"Jackson found you and dropped you off."

"Jackson brought me here?"

"Yep," Doug answered.

"He's a cop. Why the fuck didn't he take me to the hospital? Did he say how he happened upon me - out of his jurisdiction?"

"He said he was shopping with his wife and ran across you in a parking lot. He said there were two young men attacking you. He didn't say anything about Dickie being with you. Jackson told us that he ran the two boys off before they did any major damage. He drove you home in his car."

I rubbed my head and tried to sit up again. This time I was able to make it to a sitting position. I leaned against the back of the couch. "And you believe this bullshit story? Dickie was there; I swear; he was there. It was Dickie who did this to me."

"I'm not going to let you accuse your brother of this," my mother screamed at me and began shaking her finger in my face. "Your brother has always been good to you. How can you turn on him like this?"

"Because he did this, Mama," I screamed back. "He called me out there, tried to get me to sign some bullshit paperwork, and then kicked my ass because I refused to sign. Your son, my brother, did this to me. You can believe what you want, but he's a piece of shit."

And she slapped me across the face. My face already felt like someone had taken a meat tenderizer to it, so when she raised her hand to hit me again, I grabbed it. "I know you love Dickie, Mama. But I'm not going to let you hit me again. Dickie did this to me. Plain and simple."

Mom jerked her arm free, stood, and stormed out of the room. I turned back to Doug. "He did this. And Jackson just happened to find me. I hope you don't believe that bullshit."

"Look, you need to get some rest. Tomorrow will be a long day for all of us. Honestly, Bobby, Jackson said he didn't see Dickie."

"And it hasn't occurred to you that maybe Jackson is involved?"

"Why would Jackson want to way-lay you? It doesn't add up. You don't have anything that he would want."

"I'm not so sure, but I aim to find out. Somehow he's in cahoots with Dickie. I don't know his angle, but there's an upside for him. By the way, where's the Chrysler?"

"Denise and Stephanie went to pick it up. Jackson gave them the keys."

I looked at my watch. It was almost 12:30. "I'm sleeping downstairs tonight."

I got up from the couch. My first few steps were a bit wobbly, but as I made my way across the living room toward the kitchen - on my way to the basement - Harry's bedroom door opened, and Mama stepped out of the room into the hallway. She stared at me and for a few seconds, our eyes locked on one another.

Without a word, she walked toward me and turned and went into the bathroom. She slammed the door behind her. She was unyielding in Dickie's defense.

I guessed that I had committed my final act of treachery. There would be no getting along with her now. I went to bed. I needed to rest so that I could get an early start. Tomorrow promised to be an eventful day.

DAY 7 – MONDAY

On Monday morning, I got up very early before anyone was stirring. I went into the bathroom and got my first look at the damage Dickie had done to my face. I had a few bruises on my cheek and under my left eye, but overall, I couldn't see anything that wouldn't heal quickly. So, I showered, dressed and went to the basement and packed my duffel bag. I needed to get the hell out of this house and had decided to check into a hotel before the funeral.

Carefully stepping around the snoring and slumbering bodies sprawled throughout the room, I returned upstairs, grabbed both sets of car keys, and left the house. It was just 5:00 am and the neighborhood was deserted.

I threw my duffel into the trunk of the Malibu, jumped in the car and pulled away. As I headed down the street, I saw that the sun was beginning to lighten the city. I was relieved because I had feared that rain would somehow spoil Harry's funeral. Based on the beginnings of the morning, it looked as though it was going to be a beautiful and fitting day, for Harry's farewell.

I was still pissed from the night before. My mother had solidly climbed behind Dickie. It was as though I didn't matter to her. And while my family, as a whole, remained agnostic about the situation, I knew that they were leaning towards defending Dickie, as well. When it came to family, we had a way of defending bad behavior by simply shrugging it off with one phrase, "You know how Dickie is." And I was tired of the bullshit.

My stomach growled. At this time of the morning there was only one place opened for breakfast – the Drop-In Grill – on the south end of town. It was just off the highway, so a lot of truckers would stop in for an early-morning bite to eat. They were usually joined by the older folk. When Harry was alive and found it difficult to sleep, he often frequented the restaurant.

And actually, on the few occasions that I had been there, I enjoyed the meal and the conversation. It wasn't unusual for the world's problems to be solved over a good breakfast and a cup of coffee.

The crowd was still a little sparse when I went in and had a seat. I picked up the menu and looked it over. "Just some scrambled eggs and sausage," I told the waitress.

"Links or patties?"

"Links. And toast. No coffee, just a cola." She left and I sat for a moment, contemplating the day's upcoming events. But before I could fall too deeply into my thoughts, someone sat at my table in the seat across from me.

I looked up not knowing what to expect; and to my surprise, I saw someone who I instantly recognized. It was the man who identified himself as Jimmy's father, Brad Bushe, and the one that Jackson believed was Jimmy's uncle.

"May I join you?" he asked. "I'll even buy your breakfast."

I was a bit leery, but, after the past few days I had come to expect the unexpected. So I agreed to the company but was anxious to find out why he was sitting across from me. So I asked, "What do you want?"

Before he could answer the waitress returned and took his order. While talking to her I took the time to measure him up. Behind the wrinkles, gray stubble and thinning hair, I could see Jimmy. When the waitress had left, he smiled and turned to me.

"I think we need to...shit, what happened to your face?" he asked.

"Family disagreement. You were saying?"

"Remind me to never piss off your family. Anyways, I was saying that I think we need to talk."

"About what?"

"About this and that. But first of all, please accept my apologies for leaving you and your friends so abruptly. I didn't mean any harm by it, but when I saw that one of your companions was Jimmy's girlfriend, I had to excuse myself. It's a bit embarrassing meeting your son's girlfriend when you've not been a part of his life."

The waitress brought my coke and his coffee.

"The police identified you as Jimmy's uncle, not his father."

He laughed. "By police, I assume you mean Jackson?"

"How did you know?"

"Because when he came to visit he kicked the shit out of me and told me to get the hell out of town. The next thing I knew I was lying on the kitchen floor, bleeding from the back of my head while Jackson tossed the entire apartment."

"Did he say what he was looking for?"

"Not a word. He shouted some instructions to his goons, but I was too groggy to make out anything."

"Goons? Are you saying Jackson is dirty?"

He laughed. "You make up your own mind. Let's just say he sometimes doesn't operate within the book."

That didn't surprise me. Most effective cops sometimes stepped outside the rules. To me, that's what made the justice system work.

"So, when you saw us, why did you evade us and clear out?"

"There were some questions that you and your friends were going to ask that I wasn't prepared to answer. And I didn't know if I could trust you. After all, you could have been someone linked to Jackson. And that wouldn't have been a good thing for me."

"Well, we definitely wanted to know why you were there," I said.

"Yes, I'm sure you did and of course, the other obvious question – had I seen Jimmy?"

"So now that we are sitting here and male bonding, why don't you offer an answer to both of those questions?"

"Fair enough," he smiled, took a sip of his coffee and continued, "The first question is easy. I was there because I wanted to see my son. I've never been a part of his life and then one day I woke up and realized I needed to spend some time with him. So I dropped in. Jimmy didn't take it well…"

"Wait, so, Jimmy was aware you were there?"

"I know that I told you that I had just arrived, but I've been staying with Jimmy for nearly two weeks."

"He never mentioned it to me."

"Would you expect that from Jimmy? He is as hard as I am. We had a knockdown, drag-out fight, but eventually we came around, and I believe we are now bona fide father and son."

"So, have you seen Jimmy the last couple of days? He seems to have simply vanished."

Brad Bushe frowned. "Not recently. Jimmy was involved in something that he wouldn't talk about with me. He left the house one day, and I haven't seen him since. I'm afraid, based on the visit from Jackson, something has happened to him. I've looked everywhere for my son and just can't seem to find him. And since you haven't seen him, I don't know what my next move is going to be."

"No, sir, I haven't seen him or heard from him. And as far as I know, Vivian hasn't seen him either."

Brad Bushe shook his head and looked saddened by my words.

"Why do you think something has happened to him?" I asked.

"I'm not sure. Jackson was almost in a rage when he came by the duplex looking for Jimmy. I somehow had this feeling that when Jimmy left the other day, I'd never see him again. I've have finally reconciled with my son, and now he's missing. It is a difficult thing for a father."

"With all due respect, sir, life was a bit difficult for Jimmy without a father being around," I added.

"Yes, you're correct. I know things were difficult for Jimmy, and I will spend the rest of my life regretting that I wasn't a good father to him."

"So, what now?" I asked.

"I'll stick around for a few more days, provided Fred Jackson does run me off and then, if Jimmy doesn't show up, I'll move on."

We talked for a few more minutes about less important matters. The waitress brought our breakfast, and for some reason, what had been an easy conversation, became very difficult for me. I didn't have much of anything else to say to him once he had told me that he hadn't seen Jimmy.

148

I understood this father's feeling and even Vivian's sense of loss. However, I didn't believe for one minute, despite what Brad Bushe or Vivian felt, that Jimmy was dead. In my heart, I felt Jimmy was somewhere alive, but just keeping low until whatever he was running from had been worked out.

We finished our meal, and he paid the waitress. I was a bit impatient, and I think he sensed that.

"Well, I'll let you get along with your day. When I saw you sit down, I just wanted to come over, apologize, and ask if you had seen Jimmy." He looked around the restaurant. "I used to eat her nearly every day when I lived here."

"Well that's nice, Mr. Bushe. And it was great to see you again, but I have to go. I hope Jimmy turns up soon," I said restlessly. I was ready to leave.

Jimmy's father stood up and shook my hand. "Bobby, I appreciate you spending time with me. I enjoyed our conversation. If you happen to see Jimmy, let him know that I'm worried about him."

"I will. Take care, sir," I ended. But before I walked out of the door, he gently grabbed me by the arm.

"Listen, you be careful with Fred Jackson. He's a motherfucker. I have known him for many years, and I can honestly say if there's good in him, I haven't seen it."

"I'll I keep an eye on him," I said. Since the parking lot incident, I had also been suspicious of Jackson. Though Fred had been around my family and always been decent, now, I wasn't so sure about him.

He smiled and said, "And based on those bruises, you need to keep an eye on your family. Sometimes family can do you wrong, and we think it's okay because they're blood. Just because someone is related to you doesn't justify them treating you like a dog."

"Thank you, sir," I said, and shook his hand and left. His words rang true in my heart. And they, along with the anger inside of me, motivated me to commit my first act of defiance. I left the restaurant and headed for my lawyer's office.

***

149

I caught Zigelhofer at 7:00 just outside his office. He was carrying a cup of coffee and had a newspaper crammed under his arm as he fumbled for his key.

He was surprised to see me so early.

"Bobby, how are you today?"

"I'm fine, Tom," I answered. "Big day, today."

"Indeed. I plan on being at the funeral. I just have a few things to do here at the office," he said and opened the door.

I followed him in and sat down. Zigelhofer sat his things on the desk and took a seat. "What can I do for you, Bobby?"

"Two things, Tom. For one, the house that I inherited in Atlanta, I want you to put it up for sale. If we can't find someone to buy it in a reasonable time, you can sign it over to a charity in that city."

He pushed his chair back from the desk and said, "Bobby, this is real estate. It can be a significant asset for you. Why don't you just hold onto it for a while and then decide later. This is pretty sudden."

I already thought about it. Chandra was screwing me for one reason and one reason only. And had Dickie or Doug been the beneficiary of Harry's estate, I had no doubt that she would have slept with either one them. "Tom, I want to sell it. I'm not going to move to Atlanta, and I don't want to be responsible for real estate taxes down there."

"How long do you want me to have it on the market before you sign it over?" he asked.

"I don't want it to cost me anything. So at the point it begins to cost me money, I want to be rid of it."

Tom sighed. "Okay, Bobby, if it doesn't sell by the time the annual property taxes are due, I'll sign it over to a deserving charity in the Atlanta area. You'll need to sign some paperwork for me to make this happen. I know some real estate agents here, and maybe they can give us a contact or two in the Atlanta market."

"Thanks, Tom."

"You mentioned two things. What else can I do for you?"

"I need you to prepare eviction paperwork for my mother."

Tom almost dropped his coffee. "Bobby, are you shitting me?"

"Tom, I'm serious. I need you to have the paperwork ready and give it to me before the funeral. I want them out of the house in thirty days."

"Bobby, this is your Mom. She's good people. I can't prepare eviction paperwork for her."

"Are you her lawyer or my lawyer?"

He scratched his head. "Of course I'm your lawyer. But what you are asking me to do is highly irregular. What would Harry say?"

I laughed. "He would ask me why I waited nearly a week to serve her with the papers."

I was at my limit with my mother and most of my family. Lately, their actions were over the top, especially Dickie's and Mom's. Before all this had happened, I had pretty much decided to sign the house over to her. But the way she treated me, killed any desire I had to be benevolent toward her. I always felt that I would be able to take the high road, when confronted with difficult dilemmas, but the way I had been treated by my family, was eating me up inside. I just felt as though I wanted to get even.

"Bobby, can I ask you why you want to do this?"

"Mom's been upset about this whole inheritance thing. She's been pretty shitty toward me. So I decided to keep the property myself."

"And where will your mother go?"

"She still owns two houses here. She doesn't need a third. I think I'm justified in what I'm doing."

"Bobby, to me, this sounds like revenge."

"At this point, I really don't care. I want to throw all of them out."

"Is there anything that I can do to change your mind?"

"Just prepare the paperwork. I want to give her the documents right after the funeral."

"Bobby, with all due respects, I'm surprised that you, of all people, would do something like this. However, it's your property."

"Thank you, Tom. And one last thing, my sister Laura, she has some college loans. I want to pay them off."

"I don't have anything to do with that. If you want to pay her loans off, go to the bank and withdraw the money. I don't need to be involved with that."

"Yeah, I guess you are right. I just thought you might want to know…"

"What difference would that make to me? You are kicking your mother out of your step-father's house. If you need to reconcile your guilt by paying off your sister's college loans, then that's your business. Look, I'm just your lawyer. I have given you my best advice. I get paid for my time. Beyond that, you'll have to deal with your conscience yourself."

Tom was succinct and to the point. I'm not sure what I expected to hear. "Please bring the papers this afternoon, okay?"

"I'll have them for you. Now, if you'll excuse me, Bobby, I have some other work to do. I'll see you later at the funeral."

I sat there and waited as though he was supposed to say something else. But he didn't look up. I left. I had to go to the mall and buy a suit.

***

I was twenty-four years old and looking at myself in the mirror, dressed in the first suit I had ever owned. When I was in high school, I had my senior class photo taken in a sports jacket that I had purchased at a thrift shop. I had never owned a suit.

I had checked into the hotel to get ready for the funeral. I had no intentions of going back to the house this morning. Dealing with the family this afternoon would be enough for me.

I sat at the edge of the bed and reached into my duffel and pulled out Harry's notebook. It was a small, brown pocket notebook, with the word "memorandum" embossed in gold on the front cover. I opened it up and leafed through its worn pages.

Harry had all types of notes in the book. I looked over some of the phone numbers and addresses he had written down and concluded that Harry was quite the lady's man before he married my mother. The book was filled with all kinds of interesting tidbits from lawn care notes to how to replace traveler's checks.

I didn't see any type or note or explanation as to why he committed suicide. I guess I really didn't expect him to pull out his notebook and jot down his last words before killing himself. But I had to be sure.

As I made my way to the end of the book, one entry caught my attention. It was a bank account number for a bank in Atlanta, Georgia. Jotted next to the account number were the words, "money for maintenance."

So, apparently Harry had set up some type of account that he could access when he was in Atlanta for the care and maintenance of the house. And I think this is probably what his brother was after. So, it all made sense as to why Paul would want the book. He needed the account number.

There was a knock on my door. I looked through the peep hole. It was Laura.

When she came in she stopped for a moment to admire my new threads. "You're looking good, Bobby. You look nice in a suit."

"Thanks, Sis," I said.

She took a seat on the bed. "Boy, you must have been really pissed off to get a hotel room. I know Mom was pretty tough on you. I've spoken to her about it, but you know Mama."

And there was that phrase - that excuse again. "Laura, why do we always defend bad behavior? Mom was brutal with me. She said some things to me that I wouldn't say to my enemy. Mothers don't tell their children they should have drowned them. Mothers don't show favoritism toward one child. Good mothers don't do that, Laura."

"Correction, Bobby, perfect mothers don't do that. However, real mothers sometimes make mistakes. Our mother is no different."

"You say that because you aren't on the receiving end of her bullshit. I am. I didn't ask for any of this – the houses, the money, or the cars. I don't know why Harry put me in this difficult position."

"You seem to revel in it."

"How is that, Laura? This whole thing is driving me crazy."

"I say that because if you didn't want to be in this position you could have simply signed everything over to Mama, or gave it away to charity by now. But you are still holding on to it. I think in some ways you are enjoying this. I don't know what's going on in your head, but my brother Bobby wouldn't run to a hotel to get away from his mother. He would stay there and fight her toe-to-toe. And he would never, ever, stop loving his mother. Not my brother, Bobby."

"Things are different, Sis," I said to her. She was angry with me.

"How is that, Bobby? Because you have a few fucking dollars? That's no money to be tripping over. In the whole scheme of things, it's nothing. Don't let a few thousand dollars spoil your relationship with your family."

"Look, I didn't call you over here because I wanted to debate this. I asked you to come for another reason."

"Well, whatever it is, we need to get on with it. Calling hours start in forty-five minutes. So we have to get moving."

"How much are your outstanding loans?"

"I owe about fifty-three hundred dollars, why?" she asked.

"Because I want to help you pay them off with this money from Harry. Here's a cashier's check for five thousand dollars. I'll get the rest to you later," I offered.

She smiled and gave me a big hug. "Oh, Bobby, I can't believe that you are doing this. You are so sweet. Wait until I tell Mom. She is going to be so pleased that you have changed your mind about everything."

"What are you talking about?" I asked.

"I assumed you're going to sign the house over to her."

"She doesn't need any more houses. She already has two," I reminded her.

"Bobby, those houses are old and run down. You wouldn't want Mom to stay in those decrepit places. She needs a more comfortable place to live. Why wouldn't you want her to have the house? You don't need it."

"I may need it. I'm having a change of heart about this home ownership."

"Okay, then you keep the house. At least, Mom can stay there, right?"

I paused for a minute. I wasn't quite sure how to broach the subject. "Laura, don't take this the wrong way, but I don't want Mom to live in the house. She needs to move."

"Are you saying that you're going to evict your own mother, Bobby?"

I stammered for a few seconds, and then managed to mutter, "Yes, that's my plan."

"You fucker. You would throw your own mother out into the streets? You are a low-life bastard. How could you even suggest evicting your own mother? Bobby, I thought you were better than this. But apparently you aren't."

She took the check out of her purse and dropped it at my feet. "I don't need your fucking money," she snapped and walked out of the room, slamming the door behind her.

***

When I arrived at the funeral home, it was just a few minutes before visiting hours were to begin. I didn't believe that Laura had said anything to anyone because my mother had calmly met me outside before I entered.

"Bobby, where have you been? I got up this morning, and you were gone."

"I had some errands to run. I'm okay."

"Honey, things got out of hand last night. Promise me that we won't have any incidents here at the funeral home. Harry deserves a good celebration."

"Sure, Mom," I said, and walked past her into the funeral home.

As much as Spencer had turned my stomach of late, he and his staff had done a wonderful job on Harry. Sometimes we don't recognize our dearly departed when they are mocked up for the funeral by the stylist on staff. Often, it's because of the circumstances by which they left this earth. Harry didn't look like some phony figure that had been hastily dressed up. Lying there, in his coffin, he looked like Harry. And when I stared into his face, I saw a peaceful Harry. It was an expression that had somehow managed to elude his face for the last few months.

"Godspeed, Harry," I whispered to him and walked to the back of the chapel.

For the next hour, most folk in my family avoided me. From time to time, a childhood acquaintance joined me to chat, but other than that, I stood alone.

155

I was confident that Laura had not yet mentioned my plan to the family. She was pissed when she had left and thus far had avoided either eye or personal contact with me. While I was at the back of the chapel, she stayed to the front or occasionally walked outside.

I had to mend the rift between us. Laura had always been my confidante and my best friend. However, as were the other members of my family, she was fiercely loyal. In this situation, I hoped she empathized with me in some way. I couldn't expect her though, to accept what I was going to do.

The funeral started promptly at 1:00 in the afternoon. The eulogy was delivered by the pastor from my mother's church, the Reverend Albert Johnson. While he did a decent job, it was obvious that he hadn't known Harry very well. On those Sunday mornings when my mother went to church, she usually attended without Harry. He liked to watch television on Sunday and catch old re-runs of Abbott and Costello or a few Spaghetti Westerns.

From time to time, the good Reverend would stumble through a fact or two, but by and large, he kept his mini- sermon brief and to the point. When he asked if there was anyone in the family that had anything to say I waited for someone in my family to stand. No one did – nor did Harry's sister or brother.

But I wasn't going to let Harry's going home celebration precede without saying something about him. So, I stood, much to the surprise of my relatives, and walked to the front of the chapel. Even Reverend Johnson had a surprised look on his face and reluctantly handed me the microphone.

I took the microphone as Reverend Johnson whispered, "Keep it brief."

I glared at him. He quickly backed off.

"I just wanted to take a minute," I started, and suddenly felt a rush of emotion overtake me. For some reason, I found it difficult to get my words out without choking from sadness. It seemed that things had been happening around me so quickly that I hadn't taken the time to mourn my good friend. "I just wanted to take a minute," I tried again, and continued, "to just say good-bye to one of the greatest men that I have ever known."

Sitting in the back of the chapel, I hadn't really gotten a good indicator as to how many people were in the room. As I spoke and looked over the audience from the podium I could see that the chapel was full to the point that people in the back were standing against the wall. It warmed my heart to know that so many people would come out for Harry's send-off.

"If you didn't know Harry, you missed out on knowing a wonderful man. Harry believed in me and those around him. He was a good man and I'll miss him," I ended.

I handed the microphone back to the Reverend and walked out of the chapel. As I neared the door, Spencer came over to me, "Bobby, you're not leaving, are you?"

"No, I just need some air. I'm going to the gravesite for the interment."

"Okay, the family is riding in the two limos behind the hearse, so be sure to line up as soon as the pallbearers...aren't you one of the pallbearers?"

"No, I left that to others. I'll be ready to go, but I won't be riding in the limousine with the family. I'll be driving my own car."

He smiled and moved on. I walked out the chapel to get some air.

As soon as I stepped into the hot afternoon sun, I saw an inappropriately dressed Eileen hustling towards the chapel door, her beau just behind her. I stepped aside as she neared the front door, "I'm not too late, am I," she huffed.

"No, it's just getting started," I lied and watched as they both ran into the chapel, at the point in the ceremony where the pallbearers walked to the front to bring Harry's coffin out.

I peeked in as they closed Harry's coffin. This would be the last time I would see his face. I realized that for the rest of my life, my memories of Harry would be preserved solely in my mind and through the few photographs that were scattered throughout the house. Turning away from the front, I walked back out of the chapel and over to the Malibu. I rested my head in my folded arms against the roof on the car and softly cried.

***

157

I was sitting inside the car, the door slightly ajar, and my left foot resting on the parking surface, when Spencer came over to me with a handful of magnetic flags. "You want to line up near the front?" he asked, handing me one of the flags.

"No, I'll stay near the back," I answered, and tossed the flag onto the seat. That's when I noticed that Eileen and her hick boyfriend were parked next to me.

"Are you in the funeral party?" Spencer asked her.

"Yes, I'm his daughter," she hastily answered.

"Then shouldn't you be in the limousine with the other family members?" She glanced over at me. "No, I'll just follow my Step Brother."

Spencer nodded and walked away.

Eileen was standing next to me. Her boyfriend had already taken a seat behind the steering wheel. I didn't want to cause a scene, but I thought the charade had gone on long enough.

"I don't know what game you are playing here, Eileen, or should I say, Ethel."

She nervously fidgeted. "I don't know what you're-"

"Oh, give it a break. I went to the Heights the other day, and visited one of your haunts. I got the lowdown on you. I may not know exactly what your game is today, but I do know this; some kind con is going on and while I don't have all the details right now, I promise you, as soon as we bury Harry, I'm going to do everything in my power to expose you and your boyfriend. And once I find out what you're up to, not only am I going to visit the prosecutor, I'm also going to make your life a living hell."

Eileen didn't say a word. She glared angrily at me and then got into her car and closed the door.

Clearly, I'd hit a nerve. I smiled, then slipped behind the wheel of the Malibu and watched as the cars snaked out of the parking lot, following the hearse. Finally, I joined the procession and Eileen and her boyfriend followed me.

Spencer had arranged a double plot for Harry at the city's official cemetery on the south end of town. I almost laughed when I thought about it. It was optimistic of him to assume my mother wanted to be buried next to Harry.

As we proceeded through the city, I continually glanced in my rear-view mirror. I could see Eileen and her boyfriend having a pretty animated conversation. At one point, I saw him slam his hands against the steering wheel and turn and yell at her.

She said something to him and then unexpectedly, they turned off the main road onto a side street, and left the procession.

I laughed. I wasn't sure why they turned off, but as I drove I began to realize that it was going to be too difficult for me to sit at the gravesite. So, I turned off as well and headed home.

***

When I pulled into the driveway, there were a bunch of cars parked outside the house, among them, Zigelhofer's old brown Cadillac. I had thought he had probably chickened out and decided not to deliver the paperwork to me.

I walked inside and he was sitting in the living room, fumbling with the remote. I immediately could tell that he was uncomfortable. Vivian was sitting in a chair next to him, doing her best to keep him entertained.

"Hello, Tom," I greeted and turned to Vivian and continued, "Hello, Vivian. It's nice to see you both."

I looked around and saw there were other people in the house, mostly in the kitchen preparing food for the ensuing crowd.

Tom stood up and reached into his coat pocket and produced a white envelope and handed it to me. "This is what you wanted. I hope you know what you are doing. Please pass on my condolences to your family," he finished and quickly walked out of the door.

Vivian got up from the couch and came over to me. "What was that all about? He seemed upset."

"Just some unpopular paperwork he needed to give to me. It's nothing to worry about," I lied.

"Shouldn't you be at the funeral?" she asked.

"Yeah, but when we left the funeral home I pulled myself out of the procession and decided to come home. I couldn't bear to see Harry lowered. So, I'm here now. When did you arrive?"

"This morning before your family left for the funeral. I thought you might be here. I came in, and your mother asked me to stay to keep an eye on things while they were gone because she said she didn't know all the people messing around in her kitchen."

"And she trusted you," I laughed.

Vivian glanced at the envelope in my hand. "I'm thinking, Bobby, that whatever is in that envelope is going to make some people either very happy or very sad."

"Yeah, it's nothing. Just let it go. How long are you going to be around here?"

"For a while. I think I will help out in the kitchen until later."

"I saw Jimmy's dad," I said, abruptly.

Vivian smiled and calmly asked, "Did he say anything about Jimmy?"

"He said that he hasn't seen Jimmy. He told me that he had been visiting with Jimmy for a couple of weeks, though."

"Jimmy didn't say anything to me about his father. It's kind of sad. I wish I had gotten a chance to meet him."

"You may still get that chance. You never know."

The screen door opened behind me. The family was beginning to file back in. Eleanor and family entered the house first, followed by my family. Chandra walked over to me and asked, "Where have you been?"

"I've been around," I answered, just as my mother walked through the door.

"So, you couldn't go to the cemetery or ride with the family?" my mother asked.

"I couldn't see myself doing that," I answered, and made a move toward the kitchen. I wanted to escape and get downstairs as quickly as possible. I wasn't ready for any type of confrontation at this point, but I feared that I may not be able to control the situation.

Before my mother could respond, the screen door opened and Dickie walked in. He had a grin across his face and was greeted by everyone, as though he was some kind of dignitary. Despite my contempt toward him, I kept my head because I knew there was no upside for me attacking him either physically or verbally. I would be outmatched on both accounts. And right now he was the popular one in the family. I was the leper whom everyone seemed to avoid.

He looked over my way but quickly turned to Mom as she thundered across the room in his direction, her arms outstretched and screaming, "My baby."

"Fuck this," I muttered and went to the basement. When I reached the bottom of the stairs, I removed my tie and crammed it into my suit jacket pocket. I sat on the couch, flipped on the television, and put my feet up on the table.

Moments later Vivian came down and sat in the chair to my right. "What happened between you and Dickie?" she asked.

"He attacked me last night in the parking lot behind the mall. No one believes that Dickie was capable of doing such a thing. Jackson brought me home."

"How did Jackson find you?"

"That's what I'd like to know. Fuck it though. Everyone is upstairs licking Dickie's ass, as though he's the Pope. Dickie does no wrong in the eyes of this family. To hell with them all."

"Gee, Bobby, I don't think I have ever seen you this pissed at your family."

"Pissed is not the word for it. I am absolutely incensed at every one of them. Viv, since I have been home it has been nothing but drama for me. I can't catch a break. Everyone, but you, seems to want something from me."

"What do you have that they want?"

"Oh, you don't know, do you? Harry left everything to me," I explained.

"No, I didn't know that. But it makes sense. You were very close to him and did a lot of nice things for him."

"Well, unfortunately, his benevolence has turned into my nightmare. I got everything, but this 'do the right thing' mentality from everyone around me has weighed me down. And since the day that I told them, all they have done is bust my balls. I was going to do the right thing, but everyone just overwhelmed me with bullshit. And so now, I can finally get even."

"Get even? And so I guess whatever is in that envelope is your way of getting even?" she asked.

"In a way."

Vivian smiled and took my hand. "This is not the Bobby I know. The Bobby I know, while he can sometimes be a jerk or an asshole, is not hateful, vengeful or greedy. You've always been kind and loving. This goes against everything that I know about you."

"People change, Vivian. You remember the old guy that used to live down the street from the house I grew up in?"

"Yeah, Mr. Paul, the drunk. You used to tell me that sometimes he would answer the door naked."

I chuckled. "Right. And do you remember I told you he had these two Collies that were both as mean as hell. And when the dogs would get loose from their chains, they would terrorize the whole neighborhood."

"I recall this, so what does this have to do with you, Bobby."

"I asked Mr. Paul one day why his dogs were so mean. He told me that they got that way because of the neighborhood kids."

"How could children make his dogs turn mean?" she asked.

"Mr. Paul told me that even the kindest animal will turn mean when someone chains it up and continually abuses it. He said the kids in the neighborhood would come by and throw rocks, bottles, anything at his dogs when they were chained in the back. Eventually, they became mean dogs."

"Bobby, you're missing one key point," she started.

"And what's that, Vivian?"

"No one chained you up. You can get away. You can avoid the rocks and abuse. I think your explanation is weak. You're going to be cruel because you want to be cruel. It's just not the Bobby I know."

She was right. What I was getting ready to do was wrong. Harry wouldn't approve of it. "Look," I started, and reached inside my suit jacket pocket. "Take this envelope, put it in your purse and when you get home tonight, burn it for me."

I handed the envelope over to her, but just as she reached out to grab it; Dickie bounded down the stairs into the room, and before I could react, snatched the envelope from my hand.

"What's this, Baby Brother?" he asked, taking it out of my grips. Vivian tried to take it from him, but it was no use.

"So, what are you trying to hide now?" he grinned, opening the envelope and unfolding the document. He read it and as he did, his smile slowly disappeared. When he finished, he folded it back, put it in his pocket and looked at me.

"You're a motherfucker," he hissed, and dropped me to the floor with a hard right to my chin. I passed out.

***

When I regained consciousness, I was upstairs on the couch. My mother was sitting across from me in a chair, holding the legal papers. I rubbed my chin and made my way up. The entire family surrounded me. The doorbell rang and Dickie yelled, "There's nobody here."

I thought everyone that wasn't family had been shooed away from the house. My eyes cleared, and I realized that Vivian was sitting next to me on the couch.

"You keep hitting me, Dickie, and quite..."

"You shut the fuck up," he cursed and made a fist and walked threateningly toward me.

"Leave him be, Dickie," my mother ordered. She looked through the papers. "So, you want me to leave? This is a thirty-day notice."

I didn't respond. But Stephanie stepped my way and quickly slapped me. "Who do you think you are, treating your Mama that way?"

"Stephanie, stop that," my mother snapped.

"He deserved it, Mama," Doug interjected.

"If he wants me out, he wants me out. This is his house, his property.

Bobby, I don't need thirty days to get out. I can be out of here tonight. All I need is a truck to load up my things."

"You don't have to leave..." I tried, but before I could get a word out, was interrupted by Denise.

"You're damn right she doesn't have to leave. You need to leave, Bobby."

Laura jumped in. "Denise, it's his house. If he wants us to leave, we have to leave. But don't believe this bullshit that he doesn't want you to leave, Mama," she said, turning to her. "Earlier today he had told me that he was going to evict you. He planned this. I wouldn't believe a word that he says."

And so it was final. The last person in the family that believed in me had deserted me. I had felt that despite her anger toward me, she would get over it and move on. But apparently I had estranged myself from the entire family.

"I don't care if he changes his mind or not. This is his house. So, we leave. We leave everything in this house that was here when I moved in. It's all his. We don't take anything that didn't belong to me before the marriage. And we get out of his place tonight," my mother insisted. "But before I do, Bobby and I need to have a chat in private to work out the other details. There's no sense in involving the rest of the family in this."

"Look, Ma, I changed my mind. I was trying to give the paperwork..."

Dickie was fuming. "I don't believe his bullshit, Mama. You can't let him do this to you. You have to take this place. Fuck him. Take the place from him. Get the paperwork drawn up, and I'll beat the fuck out of him until he signs it over to you," he screamed loud enough for the neighbors to hear.

He came over to me and put his hands around my throat and started to choke me menacingly. "You low-life asshole," he screamed, gripping me tighter and tighter. I fought as hard as I could - attempting to break his grip - but was unable to do so. Fortunately, Doug intervened and pulled Dickie away.

"Dickie, stop that now," my mother yelled. She stood and walked over to him. Just as she neared him, his arm swung out and caught my mother in the face. She tumbled onto the floor.

I ran over to her, to help her up, but on her way to her feet, she pulled away from me and fought her way over to Dickie.

"It's okay, Dickie. Calm down, baby," she said, nursing his anger and rage.

I was left sitting on the couch. *Fuck*, I said to myself and rubbed my neck.

Stephanie took Tanya's hand, and they left the room and came back a few seconds later with their bags. "I'm going to the old house," she announced and marched angrily out the door. Moments later she stuck her head back in and said, "Doug, can you give me a ride?"

"Yeah, I'm getting out of here, too," he said disgustedly and walked toward the front door.

"Wait, I'm coming also," Laura added and ran downstairs, and moments later came back upstairs with her bags. As she walked to join Doug, Denise came out of the bedroom with a bag of her own.

They walked out of the door together, leaving Dickie, my mother, Vivian and Eleanor and her clan in the house with me. I heard Doug's car start and then pull out of the driveway.

Dickie had calmed down considerably and looked over at me. "Out of respect for Mama, I won't kill you today. But if I ever see you again, Bobby, I swear; I'm going to tear your fucking head off. And believe me, this isn't done yet. Mama is going to get this house."

Dickie was obsessed with the house. I was still shaking, and his demeanor frightened me. I hurt all over, and he was the primary reason for that pain. After beating me unconscious the night before and trying to choke me today, I realized that I had no idea of what my own brother was capable of doing. And it seemed he was willing to go to any lengths to get what he wanted.

I heard a car pull up outside and thought that perhaps the girls and Doug had changed their minds and returned to the house. The doorbell rang.

Dickie turned to the door, and before he could yell his standard warning, he noticed that it was Jackson.

"Come on in, Fred," Dickie greeted, as Fred walked into the door.

"Ms. Foster," he said to Mama. Few people in town called my mother Bremen because they had known her so long as Sarah Foster. Jackson looked around the room and saw the Bremen family huddled by the doorway to the kitchen. "Ladies, gentlemen."

He turned back to me, Dickie, Vivian and my mom. "Looks like there's been some commotion up here."

"Yeah, Fred, my asshole brother is trying to have my mother evicted."

Jackson smiled at me and walked over to me. "Is that right, Bobby? You want to throw your mama out into the streets?"

"This doesn't have anything to do with you..." and before I could get my last word out, a backhand from Jackson sent me reeling onto the floor. "Shit," I screamed, "I'm tired of people hitting me."

"This has everything to do with me," Jackson yelled and pulled his service revolver. "Everything."

He turned back to Dickie. "You said this pussy would sign the house over to either you or your mother. So what's the problem, Dickie, can't you control your little brother."

"What am I hearing, Dickie?" my mother asked.

"Shut up, Mrs. Foster," Jackson snapped.

"Freddie, why would you talk to me this way?" she questioned in shock and dismay.

"I asked you to shut the fuck up," he angrily snapped at my mother.

"I'm sorry, Fred. I thought I could get him to do it. I'm sorry, man. But this isn't over," Dickie explained.

"Of course it's not over. You owe me, and I want my money now."

"You owe the money to Jackson?" I asked.

Jackson waved his gun in my face. "He owes me big, little brother," he mocked.

"So, Dickie, Jackson is the mob that you owe?" I pressed, keeping my eye on Jackson and watching his moves carefully.

Jackson laughed. "Where the hell do people come up with this stuff? I'm the loan company, son. And your brother is indebted to me."

"But what about Armand, I offered to pay the money..."

"Armand told me about your deal. He knew you didn't have the kind of money your brother owes me. So, of course, he wasn't going to take it. Your brother owes me fifty thousand dollars. Do you have that kind of cash lying around?" he sneered.

"Of course I don't have that much money."

"But," Jackson started, walking over to me, "Your idiot brother told me that he could get you to sign the house over to him. And I'm sure it will cover the debt. So, it's all very simple. You need to sign the house over to me today."

"What happens if I don't sign it over, Fred?" I asked boldly.

"If you love your brother, then you'll sign it over to me today."

When I looked over at Dickie, I saw the real Dickie – a low-life user, whose only concern was for himself. I turned back to Jackson. "So I guess I don't have much of a choice."

"Bobby," Dickie said, "just sign it over to him. Please, shut up and sign it over to Fred."

Fred laughed. "How much did the old man leave you, Bobby?"

"Dickie owes you fifty grand. Like you said, the house should cover that amount. It's free and clear – no liens or encumbrances. Anything else is our business, Fred," I said.

"Oh, it is. I asked you a question, and I expect an answer. How much did the old man leave you?" he snapped, and moved threateningly toward me.

"Leave him alone, Freddie. This is between me and you. I owe you the money, not my family. You said that if he agreed to sign the house over to you, then we would be square," Dickie pleaded.

"Shut the fuck up," Jackson ordered and took his revolver and pressed it against Dickie's temple. "I want it all. Do you understand? I want every god damn dime of it. That's the price for your life."

"You gave your word, Fred," Dickie grimaced, his eyes fixed on the gun.

"And so now I'm changing my word. I want every fucking dime. You understand? Tell your brother to answer my god damn question. How much money did the old man leave you?"

Dickie looked over at me, his face contorted. Jackson pressed the gun against his temple with more force.

There was a pop. It was a strange pop, sounding as though a firecracker had just gone off. In fact, it was similar to the same sound we heard the afternoon that Harry had killed himself.

This sound caught us all by surprise as well, especially when Jackson's eyes rolled back into his head, and he slumped to the floor, his revolver falling at his side. Moments later, blood spilled from underneath his head. He lay still on the floor. Jackson was dead.

At that moment, I finally realized what had happened to Harry's .25 caliber Colt revolver.

***

Mom came down the front stairs of the police station. I jumped out the car and helped her into her seat. She had been a little rattled earlier when they arrested her and took her away. However, she seemed calm now.

"So what's the verdict?" I asked her, helping her into the car.

"Get in the car, Bobby, and then we'll talk. You know we don't discuss our business on the street." She was still Mama – stern and disciplined.

I closed the door, jumped into the driver's seat and started the Malibu. We pulled away from the police station, headed for home.

"They were investigating Jackson on something called Ricky, I think."

"I think you mean he violated the RICO act, Mama. So he was in deep. So what about you?"

"Well, they are going to let the grand jury decide, but since they let me out on my own recognizance, I should be okay."

"Do you know this for a fact?"

"The chief told me not to worry, so I'm not."

"And what about you mentally and emotionally? You killed a man."

"I'm okay, son. He threatened Dickie. When he put that gun up to my child's head, well, he made his bed."

"While you were in the jail, I went over to Zigelhofer's office to see if he could find someone who would represent you. Prentiss is your best bet. Zigelhofer doesn't practice criminal law anymore."

"I don't think I'll need a lawyer, but I'll call Prentiss tomorrow."

"You should hire a lawyer, Mama; it will be for the best."

"If you say so, son. Do we still have company?"

"No, the folk from Georgia left. I'm sure they were extremely upset by what went down in the house, but I also think that they were a little pissed at me."

"Why would they be angry with you?" she asked sarcastically.

I ignored the question. We rode in silence for a few more minutes. When we were about a block from the house I asked her, "So, Mama, what about us?"

"You're my child and I forgive you. We're okay."

It wasn't exactly what I wanted to hear, but I suspected she would take this position. I accepted it. That was who she was and that would be the best I would get from her.

"You know, Mama, something is bothering me about the events from this afternoon."

"What's that, honey?"

"Why did you have that gun on you in the first place?"

She turned to me, gave me a slight glare, then turned away and fixed her eyes on the road. She never answered.

***

When we arrived home, the entire family was there to greet Mama. It was a somber greeting because of the tragedies that had occurred in the house. But they were all there, to give their support. Vivian had gone home. And surprisingly, Dickie was on his knees trying to scrub Jackson's blood out of the carpet.

Initially, there was very little conversation, or any interaction, among us. But after a while, we came around, and despite the sadness, it was business as usual.

Stephanie approached me and asked, "Have you decided on the car?"

During the time that my mother was in jail, I had actually decided to sign the Malibu over to Stephanie. It was the newer car and she really did need reliable transportation to get herself, Mama and Tanya around.

169

"I'll keep the Chrysler and you can have the Malibu," I said and watched as she choked, cried briefly, and gave me one of her weak, disingenuous hugs. It didn't matter to me. A hug was a hug.

Laura came over. "Sorry about earlier," she said.

"No problem. We're cool," I assured her.

I sat down for a few minutes to catch up with everyone and to resolve a few outstanding matters. This was my family, good or bad. I just had to come to that realization and to move on.

I got up from the couch and walked over to Laura. It was just a few minutes past four o'clock.

"Can you do me a favor and drop me off at the auto repair shop?" I asked her.

"Sure, not a problem," she agreed. I tossed the keys to the Malibu to her.

"Are you sure this is okay with the new owner?" she asked.

"I'm sure Stephanie won't deny me a ride to pick up my car."

Laura laughed, and we left the house.

We got into the car and pulled away.

"Awful busy day, huh," she said.

"It was an awful sad day, Laura - one that I want to forget as soon as possible. It was a tragic day."

"But it ended well for Mama," she said.

"It did, but you realize she shot a person in the living room, point blank, in the head? So, while it turned out well for her for now, right or wrong, a man was killed. So I think it was an awful day."

"Okay, okay. Don't be so sensitive," she said.

We rode the rest of the way in silence and finally Laura pulled the Malibu into the repair shop parking lot. "You want me to wait?"

"Nope, I'll be okay. I'll call you later."

"You're not coming back home?"

"Not tonight," I said and jumped out the car. I walked to the shop entrance.

Laura called to me before I entered. "Are you ever coming home?" she asked.

I shrugged my shoulders and walked inside.

***

The repair shop did an excellent job on the Chrysler. It was in tip-top shape. Earlier in the day I had stowed my duffel in the trunk of the car before taking it to the shop. After picking the car up I tossed the vehicle registration into the glove compartment and noticed a small brown envelope inside. I opened it up and found the missing key to the safe-deposit box. I smiled and went directly to the bank.

I have to admit that when I opened the safe-deposit box, I was a bit nervous. I didn't know what I would find. Inside there were the usual valuables– some jewelry, including Harry's retirement watch and about ten thousand dollars in saving's bonds. There were a few stock certificates but nothing really major.

At the very bottom of the safe-deposit box was a note, scrawled in Harry's barely legible handwriting that simply read, 'make good choices'. It was the only communication that Harry had left to me. For the remainder of my life, I was destined to wonder about the circumstances that prompted his suicide. However, his note provided me with some comfort.

And upon putting the note back into the safe-deposit box I was reminded of my responsibility. I had one last errand to run before I could leave town.

***

When I pulled up to Vivian's house, I didn't think anyone was home. The driveway was empty. Both cars were gone. I was a little disappointed when I got out of the car.

I knocked on the door and waited. A few seconds later I heard someone come down the stairs and open the door.

"Hey, Bobby. I'm sorry I left, but I needed to get out of there. That was just too much for me to handle."

I smiled. "Not a problem, Viv. I understand completely."

"Come on in," she offered.

171

"I'm good here. I won't be long. I just needed to say a few things to you."

"What's on your mind?" she asked.

"You remember last summer when we broke up and then Jimmy starting dating you?"

"Yes, of course I remember."

"Well actually Jimmy bullied me aside and persuaded me to break off our relationship so that he could pursue you."

"I knew that. He told me the whole story. The things you guys do," she said.

"Well, I just wanted to tell you that I should have fought for you. Every day that goes by, I regret that decision. Vivian, you are worth fighting for. I should have fought to keep you."

Vivian kissed me. "Wait here."

She ran inside the house, and a few minutes later emerged with a suitcase. I took her bag and put it in the trunk. We both got into the car.

Vivian turned to me and asked "So, where're we going?"

"Away," I answered and put the car into drive.

EPILOGUE

A few days after the incident, the Grand Jury met and decided not to indict my mother. Jackson was dirty, and I guessed that the police department felt that a trial would bring only shame and embarrassment to the department.

My relationship with mom was never the same again. She passed away ten years after Harry's suicide. During our final ten years together, we often spoke, but never lovingly. Our relationship was forever strained. She stayed on in the house, but I retained ownership. After her death, I had the house sold and the proceeds split between my sisters and brothers.

No one in my family ever heard from Harry's relatives again. Apparently, they returned to Atlanta and accepted the things as they were. When I checked with the bank in Atlanta, the account referenced in Harry's pocket notebook, only had two-hundred dollars in it.

And the alleged daughter, Eileen, never again surfaced. So, I suspected it was a scam all along.

Dickie returned to Chicago. He continued his Dickie ways and fell back into his destructive lifestyle. He managed to burn through his share of the house money in a matter of weeks. I have spoken to him three times since the day my mother shot Jackson.

My other brother, and my sisters, stayed in contact with me throughout the years. They have all gone all with their lives and have a number of children between them.

Jimmy never surfaced. He was officially listed as missing. I believe that Jackson had something to do with his disappearance. But I don't think I'll ever know for sure.

And Vivian and I? Well, that's a story for another day.

ABOUT THE AUTHOR

Alonzo Heath is also the author of *The Braun Secret* and *The Booster*. He lives outside of Houston, Texas and can be reached via his website at www.lonnieheath.com.

Made in the USA
Columbia, SC
23 November 2021

49654640R00104